GIANT-SLAYERS

Giant-Slayers

PHIL WEAVER
Edited by Frances Grant

KINGSWAY PUBLICATIONS
EASTBOURNE

ISBN 0 85476 371 6

Designed and produced by
Bookprint Creative Services
P.O. Box 827, BN21 3YJ, England for
KINGSWAY PUBLICATIONS LTD
Lottbridge Drove, Eastbourne, E. Sussex BN23 6NT.
Printed in Great Britain.

To Helen, Nathan and Matthew.
Three giant-killers of the highest order.

Contents

Acknowledgements 9
Foreword 11
1. An Encounter with Giants 15
2. Giants in the Land 31
3. King of Kings—and Giant of Giants 49
4. A Job for the Weak 67
5. Giant Negative: (i) It's Personal 85
6. Giant Negative: (ii) It's Corporate 101
7. The Winning Mentality 117
8. You Too Can Win 135
9. Don't Quit 153
10. What Stops Us Setting Goals? 171
11. Setting Goals: A Very Practical Weapon 189
12. Spiritual Weapons: Slay Your Giant 205

Acknowledgements

Over the years there have been many friends, acquaintances, family and staff who have supplied me with information and inspiration, who have enriched my life and made this book possible. However, there are a few people who have made significant contributions to whom I would like to give a special mention.

First of all I would like to express my love and thanks to my wife Helen who has been my encourager and best friend for the last twenty years or so. As well as making many thoughtful suggestions, she typed and retyped the manuscript tirelessly. And this in addition to her regular responsibilities really highlights her servant heart. Her contribution has been invaluable and without her I wouldn't have been able to complete the project. In fact, without her I wouldn't be able to do very much at all! I love her. Undoubtedly she's one of God's special people, as are my two sons, Nathan and Matthew, and I would also like to say thank you to them. You will see as you read the book they have provided me with a reservoir of illustrations. Indeed, two Giant-Slayers of the highest order.

Next I would like to thank my editor, Frances

Grant. She is so easy to work with, great to know and full of life. Her ability to cut through the issues, pinpoint the objectives and remain focused has helped me to be more concise and effective. Her skill and availability in discussing thoughts, ideas and concepts have been thoroughly helpful. Her constant encouragement has been a major source of blessing.

Then there's my very good friend J. John who is always such an inspiration to me. He is so full of God. Jesus oozes out of every pore of his body.

I would also like to thank Richard Lee, Milly Murray, Guy and Gail Miller, Ed and Mary Matthews, Tim Stokoe, and of course the infamous Jacky 'Ooze' Renahan for all their ideas, thoughts and encouragement.

And to the most famous, willing and prolific contributor of all, the world-renowned 'Anonymous'—a heartfelt expression of gratitude. To all writers, speakers, teachers, preachers, philosophers, friends and people on the street—your contributions have been monumental and I'm extremely grateful.

As the late Les Dawson put it, 'I would like to thank all those who over the years never believed in me. Thank you so very much for all you have done in forging the sword of my determination.'

Lastly and above all I want to thank the Lord Jesus Christ for being my constant Companion, Saviour and Friend. I owe him everything. It is he who enables me and indeed all of us to be Giant-Slayers.

Phil Weaver

Foreword

This book introduced me to a family I have been acquainted with and affected by, but never actually been introduced to: the Giant Family. The strange thing is that when I met them I recognised them as part of my own life. I think you will too. These are the giants that roam through our lives, our churches and our world. Phil Weaver does us a great service in identifying them. This book is a booming voice to wake us up before we get trampled to the ground. Phil has eyes to see the giants and introduce them to us: the giants of criticism, bitterness, unforgiveness, pride and guilt; their brothers and sisters shame and jealousy; their cousins meanness, loneliness and doubt. This book is full of stark realism. We are made to face the fact that the land we live in is dominated by giants, and there is no running away. The only way is to face the giants and see them slain.

This is not, however, a call to look to the giant within ourselves and to slay the enemy single handed. Rather it is a call to rely on the God who is the Giant of giants. The God who can do anything. I know Phil Weaver well and have always considered him a giant for God. After reading this book I understand why. Not first and foremost because of his size and physical strength (and believe me he is massive!), but because he is aware of his weakness. This book is full of personal testimony of intimate battles he has fought, of painful exchanges he has had. There is no idealising of himself or us. There is no ducking the issue of the scale and the ugliness of the battles and the enemies we face. After reading just one chapter you will be aware of how tiny you are and how large the giants are. But Phil turns our attention to the God who loves to help weak people, who on their own have no chance against the things that tower over them and threaten to crush them. This is the God of David who wants to bring victory over the Goliaths in our lives. Phil is such a big man for God because he has realised just how big God is. He is a giant because he is a son of the Giant of giants.

Here is encouragement for all of us who can witness to the truth that God chooses the weak things of the world to shame the strong. Here is immense practical wisdom, tried and tested on the battlefield of life. Here we meet the men and women in the Bible who were giant-killers because of God: David, Gideon, Caleb, Nehemiah, the disciples. People just like us, who faced the same daily battles many of us face, and whose lives stand as testimony to the power of God. Because of him they became breakthrough people. Those who pursued excellence. Giant-slayers.

Sometimes teaching like this seems to stay at the level of slogans, leaving the reader with little to go on for actually putting it into practice. This book is not like that. Page after page is crammed with advice for daily giant-slaying: how to set goals, to keep going, to train hard, to be aware of all the spiritual resources that God makes available for us through his Holy

Spirit. Phil leaves us in no doubt what we should and must do if we are to survive in a land occupied by giants.

Phil Weaver stands with others from the past who have faced the reality of the journey towards heaven. The way of the pilgrim involves fighting the giants, as John Bunyan knew:

> Who would true valour see, let him come hither.
> One here will constant be, come wind, come weather.
> There's no discouragement shall make him once relent
> His first avowed intent to be a pilgrim.
>
> . . . No lion can him fright,
> He'll with a giant fight.
> But he will have the right to be a pilgrim.

Phil Weaver is one such pilgrim, prepared to fight with giants. This book leaves us in no doubt of that. The question is, are you? Am I?

J. John
Nottingham, 1996

1

An Encounter with Giants

'Go-li-ath. Go-li-ath. Go-li-ath.'

That name echoed through the factory, and haunted me all day long; almost everyone in the firm would join in chanting that name at my expense, for a bit of light relief to break up a laborious day. They called me Goliath because I was 6' 5" and had an ever growing girth. How I hated working there. I longed for the day when I could leave. In the event, it came sooner than I had anticipated.

It's funny when I think about working in the factory. When I was at school some of the teachers didn't rate me too highly. The type of comment I found on my school report was something like, 'Last year Philip hit rock bottom. This year he started drilling!'

In particular, I remember Wattsie, the woodwork teacher, yelling across a workbench after I had wrecked another piece of mahogany and chipped the blade of his best hand plane yet again.

'Weaver, you're useless!' he bellowed. 'The way you're heading you will never amount to anything. Goodness knows what you're going to do when you leave this place. You're really going to have to pick your socks up, me lad. If you manage to get a job in a factory you'll be lucky. Mind you, if you did you'd most probably get the sack.'

Well, I'm pleased to say I proved him wrong. I did get a job in a furniture factory and it wasn't sweeping up. On the other hand Wattsie was also right. It wasn't long before I did get the sack. That below average schoolboy and the later factory lad seemed a million miles away from the man who went on to graduate from three years at Bible college, who entered the ministry, and who now found himself with his wife and family pastoring his second church.

My first giant begins to take hold

It was some time before I realised I had a giant living with me who was hell-bent on destroying me, and it was even longer before I did anything about it. But take up residence it certainly did, and it turned out to be one of the toughest giants I've ever had to face.

We had been in the church barely four weeks when God spoke to me like a bolt out of the blue. I was well aware that God was in the habit of moving suddenly, but given what he told me this was ridiculous. I certainly wasn't expecting him to move us on. Everything seemed to be going so well, and so it should as we were still very much revelling in the so-called 'honeymoon period' of the job. Besides, didn't the apostle Paul write in Romans 11:29, 'God's gifts and God's call are under full warranty—never cancelled, never rescinded'—and God had definitely called us there. I reasoned I was suffering with a little bit of brain strain; after all it was still only 9.30 in the morning. But deep down I knew it was God. I'd got that you-know-what, I-can't-explain-it feeling.

We had moved to the church really believing God wanted us there, but it was so different from what we'd previously been used to. Many people had never left the area; life began and ended there, and that seemed strange to us. Local tradition was rich, but it was also often the order of the day. Change didn't come easy to people. In fact it was all so very different for us. Putting it bluntly, it was a complete and utter culture shock! However, we were more than excited to be in the place where God wanted us to be, and with grand visions of another great revival just around the corner we were raring to go. Little did we realise that God had other plans for the Weaver family, some of which he would share on that particular spring morning in May.

As I came down the stairs to break the news to Helen, my wife, I wondered what I could say. Walking into the living room, I said to her, 'Hey, I've just been spending some time with God and you'll never guess in a million years what he has just told me.'

Without a pause she said, 'Don't tell me we're going to move!'

'Got it in one,' I replied. 'I really do think that God is telling me that our ministry here is through and will soon come to an end. Yes, I think we're going to have to move on.'

It was hard to take it all in. All Helen could say was, 'You must be joking! I don't believe this! You've got to be joking!'

But Helen could sense I had never been more serious in all my life. I tried to show her how the Holy Spirit seemed to be showing me a glimpse of our future through my daily reading—taken from the Old Testament book of Numbers of all places. Neither of us could fully understand what was going on, but we were sure of this: if I was hearing right, then there were some very difficult times ahead.

Bitterness begins

The giant that was ready to take over my life was the giant Bitterness. I didn't recognise it then, but it grew slowly over those next few months which proved to be so particularly difficult and fraught. After our departure from that church, which finally came in exactly the way God told us it would, it really got its feet under the table of my life and made itself at home in no uncertain terms.

The crazy thing was, just before we left the church it was experiencing a good measure of numerical growth. But although things on the surface looked really good, behind the scenes it was another story altogether. For one reason or another the leadership always seemed locked in battle. If people weren't in conflict with me, they were attacking each other.

Take, for instance, the ramifications of one occasion when we decided to hold an evangelistic Sunday morning family service. We encouraged all the people in the church to bring their family and friends with them. The morning was a great success, many unchurched people came and we had a great time.

We were obviously on to a winner. My plan was to incorporate this into the church's long-term pro-gramme on a monthly basis. Who wouldn't? At the next leaders' meeting, this was high on my agenda. I thought it would have had 100 per cent backing and would go through with no problem, but I couldn't have been more wrong.

'If we have a family service every month on a Sunday morning, what are we going to do about communion, Pastor?'

I said, 'Well that's no problem. We can break bread on a Sunday evening once a month.'

Then someone else said, 'Oh I couldn't go along with that. We've always broken bread on a Sunday morning.'

'That's true,' I agreed. 'But just put the communion aside for the moment. Think about the people we could win for Christ.'

'Well as far as I'm concerned, Pastor, it's OK getting unchurched people in, but we don't want them to upset our way of doing things, do we? After all, that would be compromise.'

Then somebody else said, 'This will only happen over my dead body.'

I resisted the thought that surfaced in my mind at this point. We debated the issue long into the night, but we made no headway at all. It was like banging my head against a brick wall.

This was just one example of the leadership struggles we had, and there were many more of a similar nature. In fact, I can't remember one leadership meeting where there wasn't a major disagreement, and on many occasions someone or other would just get up and storm out. It got to the stage that every time we had a leadership meeting I felt ill through worrying about it. Somehow we never did seem to grasp the fact that as leaders we were all supposed to be on the same side. How effective we could have been for the kingdom of God, if only we'd pooled our ammunition and fired at the enemy instead of blasting at each other.

Now I don't want to suggest that it was always the leaders who were at fault and in the wrong—far from it. I was inexperienced. I didn't know how to handle matters. I would often barge in where angels fear to tread. It was no doubt six of one and half a dozen of the other, but it all slowly started getting to me, eventually wearing me down to a point where I could take no more.

Then there was a tremendous kerfuffle about Helen starting work. A lot of people didn't approve, to the extent that a prominent person in the church pulled me aside to have a quiet word with me.

'Pastor, we want you to know that there are a lot of people in the church who are not happy with Helen going out to work. You see, Pastor, a minister's wife should be doing work in the church and not outside. And not only that, Pastor, I believe you've bought a new washing machine. Those in the ministry should practise humility. Don't you think a second-hand one would have been more appropriate?'

I was completely dumbstruck. I just couldn't believe what I was hearing.

On another occasion Helen went to visit one of the leaders' wives and received a very frosty reception and was soon shown the door in no uncertain terms. I also went to visit a deacon after I'd learned he wasn't happy with something I'd done, and when he opened the door and saw that it was me, he just shut the door in my face without speaking a word.

Coupled with these sorts of incidents, there were all types of rumours flying around. What I wasn't doing was nobody's business. The whole situation was growing way out of proportion and seemed to be getting bigger and bigger by the minute. There were times when I saw glimmers of hope but just then something else would happen and the light at the end of the tunnel turned out to be an oncoming train.

It all got too much. By now I was feeling totally dejected and suffering from an acute attack of battle fatigue. Just fourteen months after taking up the post, I was on the point of what I thought was a nervous breakdown, and in the middle of a leadership board meeting (or should I say battle meeting), I quit!

The challenge

My resignation was something I later came to regret and repent of time and time again. It was not so much the fact that I had left—my time at the church was definitely finished and God had prepared me for this. What was so appalling was the way I left. Just quitting and pulling down the shutters is never God's way. Not only that, but to leave harbouring the great big giants of Bitterness, Criticism and Unforgiveness was almost professional and indeed spiritual suicide.

There were other problems, too. Finding myself without a regular salary, I inevitably ran into heavy financial difficulties, and on top of that we were living in a church manse and there was pressure to vacate this as soon as possible so the new pastor could move in. There were even threats of bailiffs, and life at home was thoroughly miserable.

As the months went by, and with lots of time on my hands, all I could do was think—and boy, did I think!

I thought about how I could get my own back. I thought that life wasn't fair. I thought that people had ganged up on me. I thought people were laughing behind my back. I thought a miscarriage of justice had been committed. I thought of leaving the ministry. It's amazing what a person does think at such times. Most, if not all, of my thoughts at that time were extremely negative.

And the more I thought, the more bitter I became and the more angry I got. I thought that God had let me down badly. My mind and heart were in a state of frustrated confusion and I couldn't for the life of me think why all this was happening. Poor old me!

Now whenever that deadly duo bitterness and anger get a grip of a person, they never just go away of their own accord, nor are they easily shaken off. In fact, they feed off one another and grow like wildfire, becoming giants that deny their victim any success, happiness or real contentment. This was exactly the state I found myself in. Wallowing in self-pity, I kept mulling the whole situation over and over again in my mind. I was for ever plotting and contriving ways of how I could get my own back. I hated seeing anybody from the church and I was quick to take every opportunity to discredit and slate anyone who I thought had hurt me, my family or my ministry and that seemed like everybody! Like most people, I guess, I figured that holding a grudge and having an unforgiving self-pity party was a good start in getting back at the folk I was angry with. I failed to see that the only person I was really hurting was me. If the University of Life had awarded degrees in bitterness and stupidity, I would have come out with a Masters!

On top of all this, I isolated myself. To my mind, it was obvious that no one could possibly understand what I was going through. I was hurting too much to let anyone get close enough to help me—I even made it hard for Helen, the person dearer to me than anyone on earth. When people tried to help, I either became like a tortoise, and totally withdrew, hiding myself in my shell just in case I was about to get stamped on and hurt again; or I acted like a porcupine, stabbing out at anyone who came near, in the belief that it was better to 'do unto others before they did it unto you'.

The repercussions of having giant Bitterness in my life were widespread to say the least. It suppressed and injured most areas of my life. The more I wallowed in the murky pool of self-pity, the more bitter and screwed up I became—annoyed with my family, the church and God. How could he have possibly put me through all this? The more I complained to God about the hand he had dealt me, and the more I gave him pieces of my mind, the more he put me on the back boiler and left me there to simmer. I simmered a lot. In fact, as the weeks went by I simmered so much, my pan became black, intensely hot and drier than dry.

I was quick to remind God that I was getting a rough deal. 'You are not doing much to vindicate me, Lord, and you're supposed to be on my side—remember?'

But God is never impressed or moved by any amount of fist-waving, foot-stomping and constant griping. The simple truth is that God never came to take sides. He came to take over.

Now giants are horrendous things. They are in their

element when they are tormenting, defying, challenging, frightening, creating havoc and causing defeat. How they like to raise their ugly heads, flex their muscles, and display their supposedly Herculean strength and dominance! My giant was now firing on six cylinders, quite determined to destroy my ministry and pretty capable of doing so. And it was at this point that the grace of God stepped in.

How God got me

Several months had now elapsed since my resignation. I was still desperately hurting, but one day I heard that a small Pentecostal church in the town was holding a special convention with a guest speaker from Scotland and I had a peculiar feeling that I should attend. The funny thing was, I had never been impressed with this particular church. It had always seemed a little aloof and exclusive, and I had never considered it 'my type of church' at all. That's why I found it strange when I had an overwhelming urge to go along—you know the type of urge: it nags and nags and doesn't leave you alone. At the last minute I gave in and decided to go. When I told Helen, she said, 'Never! That's the last place I'd thought you'd go.' But I knew I just had to go.

By the time I had driven there, parked the car and walked to the church, I was a few minutes late. As the meeting had already started I crept in and looked for a seat at the back. To my annoyance there was only one chair I could see that was available. It was right in the centre of a row and bang in the middle of the church. As I walked down the aisle I became aware that my presence created a whisper, along with a few nods, nudges and winks. It seemed as if all eyes were fixed on me. It was then that I realised that 80 per cent of the people in the meeting that night were from my old church, the one I had resigned from eight months earlier—these were the very people I was so angry with!

The penny began to drop. God had something to do with all this and I wasn't a happy man. It got worse. When you're as big as I am, i.e. mini-roundabout size, you can't slip into anywhere without causing a major disturbance. Shuffling my way past the people in the row to get to the vacant chair was a major operation in itself. I sat down feeling most uncomfortable, hot, flustered and 'got at'.

I sat there totally paranoid. I felt as if everyone knew that God was dealing with me, or at least they hoped he would! All I needed now was for the preacher to stand up and start waxing eloquent about the importance of right relationships or, even worse, the perils of a life filled with bitterness.

Then I changed my mind and began to relax a little. This was far too good an opportunity, I argued to myself, for a visiting preacher to waste on such minor issues as the personal problems of someone who wasn't even a member of that church. He would most probably want to stir the congregation, inspiring, motivating, challenging and mobilising his listeners, bringing them to a place of victory and praise. It was the right occasion for telling us that there was no condemnation in God, therefore we should go on being bold, strong and encouraged. I figured I was most probably safe—after all, it was a special convention!

But my giant was about to get its come-uppance.

When the preacher finally got up, and the congregation settled down to hear God's word, my heart did a terrifying backflip as I took in what I was hearing.

'This evening,' began the preacher in his rich Scottish accent, 'I was going to share with you about the love of God. But I really feel compelled by God to minister around the whole subject of bitterness.' Wham! God hit me, and there we were: God in the red corner, me in the blue. I thought to myself, 'This is a real set-up job if ever there was one.'

I was simply furious. Only a blind person on a galloping horse could fail to see that God had arranged all this. Who else could have got me to a church I wasn't keen on? Who else could have arranged for a load of my ex-congregation to be there? Who else could make sure there would only be one seat available right in the middle of them? Who else could get the preacher to change his sermon to exactly what I needed but definitely didn't want? It had to be God. His fingerprints were all over it. He knew there was a giant in my life that needed urgently dealing with. This was his way of making me face up to it and make a decision. I had to decide either to let go and let God have his way in my life, or remain as I was—miserably bitter, twisted, unforgiving and totally ineffective.

Being a coward, of course, I was desperate to make a quick exit, but I couldn't move. I was trapped on both sides and from above! Then, to finish me off, I heard the distinct voice of God speak into my spirit loud and clear: 'When the preacher gives the appeal at the end of the message, go to the front of the church and get prayed for. I want to deal with that bitterness in your life.'

Straight away I was on the defensive. 'No way, God. Never!'

God simply said, 'We'll see.'

'Look, Lord,' I exploded, 'get off my case! You've got me here under false pretences in the first place. You don't think I'm going to show myself up in front of this crowd, do you? If I go out for prayer, they will definitely think I was in the wrong. Besides, have you forgotten, Lord, I'm a pastor? I pray for other people, and I don't want it the other way round!'

An interesting thing had happened here without me realising it. My giant, Bitterness, had invited another giant, Pride, to join in the battle. Now tackling one giant is hard work, but when another one comes alongside then you're really up against it.

This is typical of giants, though. They often hunt in family packs, believing that if one doesn't get you another will. The Bible actually tells us that Goliath had four giant brothers. Bitterness has at least four big siblings as well. They are: Unforgiveness, Resentment, Malice and, of course, Pride. Goliath and his brothers were known as the Giants of Gath. Bitterness and its cronies had become the giants of Phil Weaver!

The dialogue going on inside of me was fast becoming very pantomime-ish. God would say, 'You have got to go for prayer. There is no other way.'

'Oh no I've not.'

'Oh yes you have.'

'Oh no I won't.'

'Oh yes you will.'

And so it went on—and on. How I wished I had some 'Go-away-God' pills on me. I would have taken an overdose!

Then I thought my next course of action should be to try a bit of bargaining.

'All right, Lord,' I said, 'I'll tell you what I'll do. I'll ask for prayer after the meeting when everyone has gone home.'

But God wasn't having any, he just kept pressing in saying, 'Just get up, go out and do what you've got to do.'

'I can't, Lord. I won't, and that's that!'

I used the name 'Lord' loosely, because when all's said and done that was what the whole thing was really about—whether Jesus was Lord or not; whether I was willing to do what he wanted!

And the giants came a-tumblin' down

The speaker was now starting to wind up his message with an appeal. 'If you have any need, especially if you are harbouring bitterness and unforgiveness in your life, then leave your seat and come out for prayer.'

The conviction of God was on me like never before. I can't explain what was going on inside of me. The giant fought back one last time.

'Lord, you're wasting your time. I'm not going out and that's final.'

But then God played his ace card.

'Now is the time, Phil. If you don't go now, your ministry is through. You are in danger of losing the lot. You'll be finished. No way will I or can I work with you in this state.'

Bull's-eye! This really hit home. The consequences of not going up were too much to handle.

'OK, Lord, you win. But I want you to know that I'm not a happy man at all.'

As the congregation stood singing a chorus, I was the first to make a move. I pushed myself out of the row and down the aisle, sensing that this is what the people wanted to see. I was certain there would be a large number going out for prayer from my ex-congregation, because I knew their hearts (or so I thought) just as they knew mine. There were many people in that room that night with bitterness and malice and unforgiveness in their lives. I got to the front of the church and the pastor came towards me. Suddenly I became acutely aware that I was the only one who had responded to the appeal. There I was at the front of the church on my own, feeling extremely conspicuous but what could I do? If ever there was a time I wished the ground would open up and swallow me, it was then. The pastor asked me what I wanted prayer for.

I told him. 'Things haven't been going so well. The thing is, I don't feel I've done anything wrong. All I've tried to do is my best. But I know I'm not right. I'm all screwed up and I'm bitter.'

Tears began to well up in my eyes as I was talking. He and the visiting preacher quietly prayed for me and I added my own quiet prayer. 'Lord, I'm in a mess. Please do something. I'm sorry.'

I can't remember what they prayed. All I knew was something lifted. God met with me. A heaviness left me and I knew, I just knew, the giant was dead. God had responded to my repentance and obedience as he always does and the job was done. At that moment in time, for me at least, it felt like every angel in heaven had burst out spontaneously in the Hallelujah Chorus!

It's difficult to explain but in a moment the giant who had gripped my life so severely came face to face with the Almighty One who was infinitely more powerful and greater than the giant—we're talking about the most high God here. The giant Bitterness was simply no match whatsoever and had to bow down.

The meeting drew to a close. The fact that people were still watching me didn't bother me any more. I left the church with a spring in my step, knowing full well that Almighty God had met with me and slain the giant. Going home in the car I felt good, in touch with God and full of praise. But there was still one thing I couldn't understand.

'Lord,' I asked, 'why weren't there more people out for prayer? What about the rest of them? Why didn't they respond?'

God gently whispered, 'Son, leave them to me. The important thing is that you responded, and that means you and I are back in business again; that's all that matters where you're concerned.'

When I got home, I walked through the door and into the living-room.

Helen looked at me in wonder. 'What's happened?' she said. 'You look quite different.'

And I was—never to be the same again. The giant had fallen!

2

Giants in the Land

Throughout God's word in the Old Testament, giants were not an unfamiliar sight. We often read of them waging war and opposing the people and work of God. They are first mentioned in Genesis, chapter 6, where it simply states, '. . . and there were giants in the land in those days.' Such giants were enormous, sometimes reaching a height of nine or ten feet. The infamous giant Goliath in the first book of Samuel is recorded to have been six cubits and a span high. Or, in other words, a massive nine feet six-and-a-half inches tall. Now that's big!

These giants clearly used their physical advantage as a weapon, oppressing the people around them. Their stature was totally intimidating, and if their appearance alone wasn't frightening enough, the very thought of doing battle with such mighty opponents must have struck sheer terror into the hearts of anyone else.

However, the underlying truth that the Scriptures give us repeatedly about giants and those they terrorised is that *God's people have the strength and the courage to fight back*. God gave them the where-withal, and made them easily capable of defeating any giants, no matter what size, no matter how strong and formidable and no matter what reputation they carried. Indeed the Old Testament proves time and time again that through God and in God, victory belongs to the people of God—even in the midst of what seems like undefeatable opposition. Moreover, this was just as true for people in the New Testament as it was for those in the Old Testament—and it is just as true today: 'Greater is he that is in the people of God than he that is in the world.'

The wrong image: giants are for real!

All too often, when we think about giants we conjure up a picture of the character from 'Jack and the Beanstalk' who stomps around fairyland with thumping feet shouting, 'Fe, fi, fo, fum.' Basically, he's a sort of cartoon character, a bit of a joke.

The Old Testament giants couldn't have been more different. They were huge in size, unbelievably strong and constantly defiant, and they mocked and stood against the armies of the living God. These giants were definitely big and unfriendly, and there was nothing stupid or funny about them. Believe me, there was nothing mystical about them either—these giants were for real!

Now there are modern-day giants that are just as real and just as determined about opposing and frustrating the purposes of God. I'm not talking about physical giants like those in the Old Testament, but about those situations and circumstances in which we often find ourselves that are too big for us to handle. Some problems are so enormous—like living in the grip of giant Bitterness as I did—that you can't see beyond them; and they are so stubborn that they just won't go away. You know the type of problems: they keep confronting you and you just don't know what to do with them. It's as if the devil himself is standing by your side mocking and taunting you, convincing you that you're in a no-win situation. Of course, there are times when you feel strong and you work up enough courage to try and tackle and deal with the problem once and for all, but before long it overwhelms you again and causes you to scurry back once more into hopeless defeat.

Giants in the land

A good example is giant Guilt—one of the biggest, in fact. Guilt tells you, basically, that because of all the dreadful things you've done, you're a worm, and it shouts things at you like, 'Call yourself a Christian!'

Guilt has a couple of tow-alongs, giant groupies if you like, called Shame and Conscience. Of course, both shame and conscience are, in fact, quite legitimate providing they spur us on to say sorry and move us on to become creative and effective for God once more. But when they just tag along behind giant Guilt, there's no getting away from them. They want us to stay a worm for ever—if not longer! That's why they all drone on, 'You're a worm so there's no point you doing anything because you're a worm so there's no point you doing anything because you're . . .'

Many of the elements which giants represent are, in small measure, useful, if we are realistic about them. If we fall back on God, our mistakes (on which the giants of Bitterness and Resentment otherwise feed) can lead us to a sober recognition of reality, and then to forgiveness; meanness can bring in a sensible element of caution; doubt can sharpen our struggle with a challenging problem; and pride can help us stand up for what is right.

But when we side-line God and such elements grow out of all proportion, they then become as giants—all-enveloping, all-focusing, totally greedy for attention. Greed itself is a giant, making for the blackest of murky territories. With its crippling companions of Jealousy and Rivalry, Greed grabs at countless numbers to fixate them with acquiring and accumulating material things. How many siblings come to grief when they start to grab at the estate left by their late parents? Can't they see the cost? Giant Jealousy ruins their potential for love; giant Rivalry puts gain before people (people are just left in the gutter); and giant Greed caps the lot with that ugly, heartless lust for 'things'. Meanwhile, relationships, and even whole lives, are sacrificed in the whole wretched process.

It is giants such as these that I address in this book. Because when a problem in someone's life has become really giant-like, a major part of living, there is actually a danger that the person will accept it as being part and parcel of life itself. Before long, they reason (consciously or unconsciously) that if they can't do anything about it, they might as well learn to live with it. The simple truth is, however, that this is anything but pleasing to God. He finds no enjoyment whatsoever in seeing his people accept defeat.

Different strategies and unfair tactics

Now giants don't always work in the same way. They have different strategies that are particularly designed to hinder and obstruct our own individual walk with God. Some giants use the short-sharp-shock method of intimidation. They throw everything they've got at you, creating havoc over a short period of time. Then they lie dormant and go into hiding and let you get on with your life again. Some time later, just when you're least expecting it, when you feel you are managing and perhaps even getting on top of things, they raise their ugly heads again and carry on right where they left off—catapulting you back into upheaval and sheer misery. It's what I call being caught in the 'stalemate syndrome'. The devil hasn't actually knocked you out, but you're not knocking him out either. Sometimes it can go on like this for months or even years.

Then there are the giants who are more creeping, more insidious, who never leave you alone. Wherever you are, whatever you do, there they are in the shadows, ever before you, using the 'all-out, no-holds-barred' approach. They have been put there to break you, causing you to lose confidence in the word of God, ultimately getting you to question your relationship with God and even doubt God himself.

The giant of Meanness is a good example here. This kind of giant wants you always to count the cost, never to give without measuring first or making some kind of bargain, never to trust, and finally to get you to the point where you say, 'What's the use of giving anything?' After all, the last thing the devil wants is for you to succeed in being truly generous, either materially or spiritually, and to win through.

Another giant in the Meanness mould is, unfortunately, often ill-recognised as a giant. This is the giant of Embarrassment. It's the one that causes you to say, 'I'm not sure what I think. I don't know what to say. I'm too shy to do anything . . . so I won't. I'm too embarrassed, so I'll do nothing.' This is an even quieter, sneakier giant who is nevertheless just as powerful and this giant too refuses to budge. It's got you so that you can't concentrate on anything else, you simply can't see beyond the problem. You wake up in the morning thinking about how you have to guard your every move, or how embarrassed you're going to be that day, and then you go to bed at night having nightmares about the same issues—that is, when you finally get off to sleep.

A third giant like this is the giant of Loneliness. God wants us all to love one another and live in harmony. But giant Loneliness makes its victims think they have nowhere to turn; that they're totally isolated; that nothing relates to them; that nobody cares. It shrinks the soul, but worse than that, it's a sheer lie.

Of course, this delights Satan and is exactly what he wants: to get you to take your eyes off Jesus and focus on the problem. When you do this, Satan knows that in your mind the problem often increases, getting bigger and stronger, while your own resilience and strength diminish, getting smaller and weaker!

Yet another giant in the same mould is Doubt. Now at this point it's important to distinguish between doubts of the mind and doubts of the heart. Doubts of the mind make up a constructive element in the human psyche. From the earliest age, a person needs to say, 'I have doubts about . . . eating sand/electric sockets/crossing the road/skipping school/losing my temper . . . because it may lead me into danger.' Doubts are necessary for every doctor and dentist in the world, so that they don't charge ahead with crazy treatments. Indeed doubts are necessary for every investigator of anything, so that a really thought-through strategy may emerge.

Doubts of the heart, however, are different, and this is where giant Doubt comes in. I remember when Helen and I married, I had plenty of doubts of the mind! I doubted where we would live, whether we'd make out financially, whether the cere-mony would go off without a hitch, and so on. But I had no doubt in my heart about Helen. When you have doubts of the heart—about whether you are loved at all, about God's place in your life, about who on earth you are in the first place—then the giant Doubt is sitting pretty in your front parlour! Like Meanness, Doubt is also an underhand, whin-ing, creeping monster that points out a problem at the slightest opportunity and tries to change it in your mind from a doubt of the mind to a doubt of the heart. The devil knows that fixing your eyes on problems will eventually destroy your faith, whereas fixing your eyes on Jesus will perfect your faith. So all his efforts are to make the problem so big that it demands your complete attention and totally pre-occupies your thinking.

You will recall how Peter, the disciple of Jesus, achieved the impossible by walking on water only as long as he kept his eyes on Jesus. But when he began to look away, at the wind and the waves in the natural realm, he began to doubt—and sink. Satan will throw everything he's got at you so that you will become negative and disillusioned, in the hope that you will finally look away and eventually throw in the towel.

So there we are. We have great, up-front giants—Fear, Bitterness, Greed, Guilt, Pride and Public Shame; and we have the 'underground', creeping giants—Doubt, Meanness, Self-pity, Loneliness, Embarrassment and Self-deception. They all work in different ways, but they produce equally horrific results. Their varied tactics have pushed many people to the point of a nervous breakdown, putting some into psychiatric units or subjecting them to a life of anti-depressants. Untold marriages have been wrecked and homes broken. Some people have even been pushed to the limit, eventually thinking life wasn't worth living any more.

At a corporate level, too, many a business has been 'eaten up' by similar sorts of giants. So have many church projects and God-given visions, all of which have been aborted and come to nothing because of 'innocent' but insurmountable opposition. One thing is for certain: giants are for real and they mean business. They take no prisoners. They shoot to kill.

Only got 'ise' for you

The worst thing about giants is that all too often you just can't keep your eyes off them. It is important to realise that the giants also have not only 'eyes', but 'ise', for you. They are determined to victimise, tyrannise, neutralise and immobilise you in your efforts for God. Now it is also important to know that it is the devil who is the master of the 'ise' and who specialises in particular in the art of 'disguise'. He is the perpetrator behind every giant, setting them against you to distract you, manipulate you, frustrate you and systematically break you down. However, there is no need to panic! God is on your side; he is most definitely for you. And if God is for you then nothing and no one can successfully come against you as you put your absolute trust in him and his word.

Characteristics and ploys of the enemy

1. Giants affect everyone

No matter who we are or what we do, we all at one time or another have to face the tough times. There are times for all of us when our backs are against the wall, when the problems of life and the opposition stubbornly stand in the way. There are times when the chips are down, and we are hard-pressed on every side.

Even Jesus was tempted in the wilderness. The only difference between him and the rest of the human race was that he was able to resist his giant (the lure of personal power) in perfect obedience to God. Jesus, of course, faced the most terrifying of all prospects at the time of his crucifixion, praying in Gethsemane, as we would have done, that he be spared the horrific days ahead. Wasn't it an incredible feat that he also added, as I suspect we would not, 'Yet your will, not mine, be done'?

This shows us another characteristic about giants:

they are no respecters of persons. They may well appear in different forms and use many different means of attack, targeting our personal, domestic and family lives. They may come against us mentally, physically, materially, socially, emotionally and spiritually, or all of these; and they can affect our financial, business, social, family, pastoral and church lives, or all of these too. But the fact remains, giants are common to all. No one, absolutely no one, is immune.

2. Giants are liars

The devil is the father of lies. He's a master at getting you to believe that you're the only one in the whole wide world who is battling with strife and struggling with life. He gives you one massive complex, getting you to believe that you must be the biggest failure that ever walked on planet earth. (This is exactly how I felt during my experience when I fought with giant Bitterness and its best mate, Pride.) Make no mistake: the devil is an out and out liar and not to be believed under any circumstances!

Jesus did warn us about this. He knew all about the evils of Satan, and warned us that '. . . in the world you will have tribulation . . .'. But he also went on to say, '. . . but be of good cheer. I have overcome the world.' So why do we believe the devil's lies and not the truth of Jesus' words? Let us see the devil's deception for what it is and say 'Hallelujah!', for again we see Jesus giving us great hope and the promise of victory over evil.

3. Giants are accusers

The devil would also have us believe that there must be something radically wrong with us personally for us to be challenged and confronted by problems in the first place. He accuses us of being hopeless, useless, feeble, afraid, weak—and we often believe it. What's worse is that such accusations can even become self-fulfilling prophecies. Yet this is another damaging lie, another complete distortion of the truth. God is, actually, genuinely merciful; he really does have the grace with which to open our eyes and see that we don't have to accuse ourselves of such rubbish.

4. Giants are crafty

The devil wants you to believe that because there is opposition, you must therefore have got it wrong and such opposition can't be 'of God'. He tells us that if it was 'of God' everything would be plain sailing. Many Christians abandon all hope because they really start falling for this hook, line and sinker.

But, if anything, opposition may well prove in reality that it *is* 'of God'. Jesus' great humanity lay in the fact that he, too, knew pain and suffering; and he, too, would much rather have avoided them. But Jesus also knew a couple of other things: first, that some trials are of God and we have to go through them; and second, that miracles can happen when we handle opposition well. In focusing his entire life on the will of God, Jesus knew this more than anyone: trials can lead us closer to God. They are the no-pain-no-gain miracles, if you like, and in them God becomes the gardener, pruning his vines so that they can bear much fruit. In other words, no one ever achieved anything without facing and overcoming negative opposition and adverse attack, and neither will you. We will come back to this later.

So the real issue is not the confrontation of the giants—this is a dead cert—but rather our attitude towards them when they do attack us and how we deal with them. Your foe, that giant, whatever kind of giant it is, will either make you or break you. You have got to determine within your heart that you're going to press on, push forward and win through, no matter what obstacles are thrown in your way.

Better or bitter?

The Old Testament character Jonah found himself in a most difficult situation, to say the least, when he was in the belly of the big fish. When you think about it, he could only have got out of his predicament in one of two ways. It was either via the mouth of the fish or . . . well, no points for guessing the other way! He could either have come out the better way or the bitter way. Sadly, many come out of their difficult times bitter and not better; defeated and not victorious. God's will is for you to come out the better and stronger person for having faced the opposition and triumphed. Make a quality decision within your spirit today that whatever you are going through, you are going to forge ahead and come out the better. You are going to be one of God's overcomers.

The God of breakthrough

Breaking through and getting the victory is never easy. However, that is exactly where God wants you to be—in the place of breakthrough. In 1 John 5:4, we are told that everyone born of God has the potential and capacity to overcome the world and all that it throws our way.

It is in the account of the classic battle recorded in 1 Chronicles 14 that God proves this. The young David had just been appointed the king of all Israel. When the Philistines heard this, they went to search straight away for David. They wanted to teach this little whipper-snapping upstart a lesson or two. Meanwhile, when David heard the Philistines were in hot pursuit he could have been excused for going into a panic, but he did nothing of the sort. He neither melted away nor ran away. He simply prepared his men to go out against them.

When the Philistines got to the Rephaim valley, David thought it was time to call a war cabinet meeting, a briefing session with his spiritual commander-in-chief. David asks God if he and his men should go up and stand against the Philistines. Basically, he wanted to know his chances of winning. He might have been inexperienced in this type of thing, but he knew that not to have God's backing would have been foolish and absolutely disastrous. It would have meant certain defeat with countless casualties. God did finally give him the go-ahead with the promise of victory, and that's all David wanted to hear!

How important it is to consult the Lord in everything, for it is he and he alone who is able to lead us into victory. Proverbs 3:5–6 encourages us to 'trust in the Lord with all your heart and lean not to your own understanding. In all your ways acknowledge him and he will direct your paths.'

The battle takes place and David and his men emerge as champions. David then makes the point of marking the victory by calling that particular place 'Baal Perazim' which means 'the God who breaks through'. David learned a lesson that day that he would never forget: even in the face of the most fierce opposition, God can and will bring breakthrough if you are careful to acknowledge him and let him direct your paths.

You don't have to lose

God is undoubtedly the God of victory, the God of success and the God of breakthrough. We as Christians can arise and enjoy that victory which God gives in Christ Jesus. The devil might well be the master of lies, but the exciting news is that we don't have to be taken in by him. We don't have to fail. We can win through if we are willing to pay the price. Oh sure, giants are for real but they don't have to threaten any individual for ever!

Let's get back to David's encounter with the giants in the valley of Rephaim (which literally means 'valley of giants'!). The exact nature of God's involvement on the battlefield that day is not recorded, nor is the precise manner in which he dealt with the Philistines. However, we are informed that God's action was sudden and devastating: 'God has broken through my enemies by my hand like a breakthrough of water' (1 Chron 14:11).

Many centuries before, Moses too experienced God's extraordinary power; Deuteronomy 33:26

states that 'there is none like God . . . who rides
through the heavens to help you . . .'. Christians today
can be certain of God's immediate help—he has never
been complacent in responding to his people's needs.

David encountered sudden victory that day
through the intervention of God in the face of
horrendous opposition. One minute he was facing
indescribable onslaught in the valley of giants and
then suddenly God broke through his inadequacy
and weakness, achieving for him a momentous
victory. It was a victory for which David was compelled to credit God, in a way that particularly
emphasises the divine action. 'God has broken
through my enemies . . . like a breakthrough of
water.'

The master of breakthrough is also the key to our
own success. Within our struggle against modern-day
giants, when the enemy presses in, we as Christians
need to be ever mindful of the indwelling presence of
the Holy Spirit, the 'Lord of breakthrough'. Such a
realisation will stimulate confidence of victory while
preventing personal spiritual brokenness.

We must be active, not passive

The fact that God broke through did not mean that
David had no part in the battle. While he was careful
to credit the victory to God's intervention, he
nevertheless acknowledged his own personal activity
within the battle. He said, 'God has broken through
my enemies by my hand.' God used David. David
physically had to face the giants. He was the one who
wielded the sword, the one who organised the
appropriate strategies and the one who stationed his

troops in their position of battle. It was 'by my hand', the hand of David, that the battle was won. None of us can be passive or inactive in the face of giants and expect to come out on top. God expects us to play our part in the battle. In doing so God not only uses our faith but our strengths and weaknesses, gifts and talents, intelligence, experience and commitment to bring about great victories.

However, when victory is secured we still need to be careful to give God the praise and glory, for it is he who gains the victory, albeit by our hand. When the donkey carried Christ into Jerusalem on that first Palm Sunday, what a foolish animal it would have been to think that all the praise and applause was for him. He did his part, but the victory was the Lord's. Make sure you give God the glory!

Beating the opposition

The giant opposition you face will either be very harmful or will prove to be extremely valuable. It is either going to defeat you or give you an opportunity to learn more about God and his victorious ways than you have ever known in your life before. Whatever your giants are, don't let them beat you. Decide in your heart that you will not draw back or give in to them. Become determined in God and stand your ground. Decide in your heart that you will rise up and not shrink back. Be determined to march forward in the name of Jesus and do whatever it takes in God to win through.

With God you are nothing less than a winner. As you put your total trust in him you simply cannot lose. In heaven's eyes there are no hopeless cases.

Whatever it is, it's never too big and never too strong, it's never too far gone, that God can't break through and work it out for his glory. In God there are no mountains too big to climb or rivers too deep to cross, for with God and in God all things are possible.

So when you face a difficult personal task, act as though it is impossible to fail; for in God, victory is assured. In other words, if you're going after Moby Dick, then be positive and take the tartare sauce with you! You are a winner, and the God of breakthrough goes with you.

3

King of Kings—and Giant of Giants

At twenty-two years of age, not long married and fresh out of Bible college, I had just been appointed pastor of my first church. Looking back I am not so sure that there was ever anyone who was so naive. Of course, I didn't think so at the time. In fact, I thought I was going to shake the world. 'Watch out, world! The new Billy Graham has arrived!' This was it (so I reckoned)—life in the ministerial fast lane! I could hardly contain my excitement. Who'd have thought it—me, Phil Weaver, a real live pastor!

It's a funny thing about having giants in your life: if you let them dominate you, the only way you can go is down. So why do we let them get to us? At this time, the giant about to tower in my own life was a giant called Lack. Of course, beginning with high expectations, that meant only one thing for me—disappointment.

There was no induction or welcome service that day. For one reason or another, it was a case of just turning up and getting on with the job. I can remember that first Sunday morning as if it were yesterday. Neither Helen nor myself could drive at the time so we set off on foot to walk the couple of miles from our new home to the church. It was a dull, overcast morning, and we walked at a frantic pace.

'Slow down a little,' Helen panted. 'There's plenty of time. What's the rush?'

'I'm sorry, love. I wasn't thinking. Truth is, I can't wait to get there. I'm so fired up, I'm ready to preach to thousands!'

When we did arrive, not even the church's old, dark, dilapidated exterior with its cracked and broken windows (facing the funeral directors and chapel of rest!) could dampen my enthusiasm. Inside was no better. Dark, dingy and very depressing would be a fair assessment of our first impressions. There were wet patches all over the rough wooden floorboards where the roof had leaked during the night. The dirty mustard-coloured gloss paint had flaked off the brick walls and there were holes in the plaster of the high-beamed, apex ceiling. The makeshift pulpit stood on a forklift truck pallet which was covered with a piece of maroon-patterned carpet.

In fact, it seemed even colder and bleaker inside than it did outside. It was like walking into a time warp and going back thirty years. I looked at Helen and she looked at me as if to say, 'What on earth have we come to?' It was hardly the revival centre of the north.

The entire congregation that morning, apart from Helen, consisted of two elderly ladies, one of whom was partially blind and the other partially deaf. Would you believe it—one could hardly hear the service, and the other could hardly see it! Who says God hasn't got a sense of humour?

Walking back home after the service I didn't know whether to laugh or cry. I turned to Helen and said,

'There must have been more life in the chapel of rest across the road than there was in church this morning.'

Helen reminded me of something I once said to God. 'Well, you did pray that God would put you in a real difficult place. What was it now? A place of challenge and somewhere you could get your teeth into and prove God?'

That prayer of mine had seemed so spiritual at the time but I was beginning to regret opening my big mouth. So don't pray prayers you don't really mean. It can be dangerous.

The giant Lack

In a pioneer situation like the one we found ourselves in, there were many giants to be faced. The biggest for us, as I've already mentioned, was giant Lack. This particular giant totally dominated every initiative and was determined to squeeze out any life that already did exist or could exist within the church. Lack was everywhere. There was a lack of people, a lack of leaders, a lack of resources, a lack of finances, a lack of workers, and generally speaking a lack of life. The list could go on. . . in short, there was a lack of almost everything. The only thing that was in abundance was Lack itself.

The small church often finds itself in the grip of Lack, and it proves very difficult to overcome. (You will find that this giant gets around a bit; it's always creeping into the life and work of the larger church as well.) Now the whole purpose of this giant is to dictate the pace by neutralising the efforts of the local church, and making it absolutely ineffective and irrelevant within its community.

Breaking Lack wasn't easy. I received no salary or expenses all the time we were there. We literally trusted God from day to day. Of course, to some this sounds quite exciting and I suppose there was a certain precarious feel to it. In reality, though, it was hard graft. But God was good and he met all our needs, and in time we began to crack it. Three years later, God moved us on. Reflecting over that time, we realised that the church had grown from just two people to a group of between thirty and forty. We didn't accomplish all that we thought we might, but the church did grow and God did teach us some invaluable lessons. For instance, he showed us how to trust him in everything. He taught us there wasn't a need he couldn't meet and he taught us he really is the God who 'specialises in things thought impossible'. He taught us in no uncertain terms about the ministry and that being in 'full-time service' and living by faith was hard work and anything but glamorous.

To believe God when life seems impossible can take every ounce of strength and faith you possess. It certainly took ours, but the results were good and we look back at our time in our first church with much affection. However, if I thought we faced giants there, they were nothing compared to the giants the apostle Paul faced when he went to start a work in the city of Corinth.

Giants in the metropolis

Corinth was a place and a half! Anything that could go on did go on, for in Paul's day it was the most important city in Greece. Historians tell us that it was a bustling hub of worldwide commerce, and a giant cultural melting pot with a great diversity of wealth and intellectual and moral standards.

It was also a place of degraded culture and idolatrous religion, and while it may well have been a key city of its time, this cosmopolitan centre thrived on financial gain, dubious entertainment, vice and corruption. It was commonly known as 'sin city', where pleasure-seekers went to Corinth to spend money on a holiday from morality!

Paul himself was honest enough to admit that even he went there feeling weak and totally inadequate, with much fear and trembling in his heart (1 Cor 2:3). He had faced some pretty big challenges in his time but this one was something else. He was going to have to draw on every last bit of his vast experience to pull this one off. It also meant that he would have to trust the one who had sent him there like never before.

When he arrived, Paul must have stood in the middle of the metropolis, wondering what God had brought him to. He knew God had put him there, and that there was a job to be done; but although Corinth had got itself a bit of a bad reputation, never in his wildest dreams had Paul thought it was this bad. Surely there were easier and more conducive places to pioneer a new church—he'd have been far safer getting a job as a lifeguard by a shark-infested sea!

Setting the scene

By modern-day standards the city of Corinth was only medium-sized, with a population of round about half a million. However, it was big for its day and extremely important—so much so that the Romans had made it the capital of Achaia. It had therefore gained the reputation of being the centre of activity and, being a sea port, was also a place of strategic significance. Consequently, it had developed into one crazy melting pot—a hotchpotch of races, creeds and languages—and it was now the meeting point of many different cultures.

A fast buck

Corinth was ideally situated for importing and exporting merchandise, making it a major centre of commerce and trade. The city teemed with all kinds of business people, residents and travellers alike, and had become extremely prosperous. Equally, it had become a city ripe for all sorts of corruption. Almost every con-man ended up working out of Corinth. It was the in-place for making a fast buck or two. It certainly had plenty of second-hand 'chariot' sales-men—you know, the type that advertise every vehicle as being low mileage, and only ever having had one owner! A giant called Corruption had definitely made himself at home in Corinth, along with a whole host of others.

The slave trade

Slave trading was big business in Corinth. Umpteen thousands of men, women and children were sold on the open market to the wealthy business folk as cheap labour—it was a case of supply and demand. The slave traders made mega-money and were accepted as important people within the Corinthian society, while slaves had no status at all. Paul realised that a giant called Slavery had a horrific stronghold in this city.

Clever giants

Corinth was also known for being a proudly intellectual city. There were many philosophers and itinerant teachers promoting their many varied speculations and theories; there were academics who were so eloquent that they could make the most ridiculous theories sound like the gospel truth; there were debaters whose wonderful rhetoric could tie anyone up in knots; and there were all kinds of theorists who could argue clearly, rationally and with great conviction, almost regardless of their subject. (In my opinion there is only one thing worse than someone talking a load of rubbish and that's someone talking a load of rubbish and making it sound like it makes sense!)

Anyway, the city was full of clever people. Even the apostle Paul couldn't match the eloquence of these high-falutin intellectuals—hence his point later that the church was not built on persuasive words or superiority of speech, but rather on the demonstration of the Spirit and in the power of God (1 Cor 2:4).

But people were basically the same then as they are today. In the end, they are less interested in fancy words and smart theories than in hearing the real, deep truth in plain language. They are looking for something that is powerful and that works in everyday life, meeting everyday needs and offering a real hope for the future. Clever debates, convincing speeches and all the theories in the world are pretty worthless when it comes to making sense of life and making it work. Paul knew this could only be found in God. He also knew that all that futile philosophical garbage would only cloud the real issues and get in the way of truth. Indeed, the giant of Artifice was yet another giant that the apostle would have to face and overcome.

Sex and religion

Religion played a major part in the lives of the people of Corinth. This was where every type of religious crank you could imagine settled. Scores of pagan temples and shrines thrived in the city, built for the glory of all manner of gods, and for the performance of various strange rituals. It was a city steeped in false religions and dominated by demonic powers.

If that wasn't bad enough, most of these cults were known for encouraging and practising sexual immorality. For instance, the city was over-shadowed by the 'Acrocorinth', a hill over 1,850 feet high. On this hill stood the large temple of Aphrodite, the supposed goddess of sex and lust. This one temple had no fewer than 1,000 priestesses—who were all prostitutes. Accompanied by the many prostitutes from other cults, these priestesses would ply their trade up and down the streets of the city every night, endeavouring to seduce the vulnerable into cultic practices and beliefs. No doubt Paul himself would have been propositioned many times.

Public morality was, of course, at a very low ebb throughout the whole of the Roman Empire. But Corinth in particular was universally renowned for its moral depravity. It was the centre for homosexuality; 'red light' areas were commonplace; and the city had many taverns from which scores of male and female prostitutes operated. Indeed, to be accused of 'behaving or acting like a Corinthian' was to be labelled with the lowest form of insult and contempt, for this was a city rife with every sexual persuasion you could think of. Giants Lust and Greed were certainly in residence there, polluting the atmosphere with their vile stench.

You can imagine that all this added up to Satan thinking that the city of Corinth was one of his greatest triumphs—an extremely secure territory that was classed as absolutely safe from ever becoming part of the kingdom of God. It was so firmly controlled by the many giants he had stationed there that there would definitely be no surrender without an all-out war!

In Paul's shoes

Now just take a minute to put yourself in Paul's shoes. What would you have done faced with such circumstances?

It was no wonder Paul stood in the middle of Corinth feeling totally bewildered. At this stage he would have been forgiven for doing a runner and getting as far away from Corinth as possible. After all, who in their right mind would want to take on a headache like this? Besides, if ever there was a situation that could kill off Paul completely, then this was the one. Surely the best route to take was the one right out of town?

But Paul didn't run, and this begs the question, why? Why didn't he head for 'Easy Street' and onto 'Comfortable Drive' where he could spend the rest of his life in early retirement making the odd tent for his garden? Why didn't he say, 'Thanks, Lord, but no thanks. I'll give this one a miss.'

The thing that tipped the balance was this. In spite of

all the discouraging facts about Corinth, Paul knew of
a vital piece of evidence which would help him win
through. He knew that the one in him was greater than
the one in the world (1 Jn 4:4). Of course, this evidence
was based not on what was visible to the naked eye,
but on what could be seen through the eye of faith. Paul
didn't see just the material facts, he also saw the spiritual ones, and he knew the situation in Corinth would
only be temporary if God intervened and transformed
that seemingly impossible environment.

Then Paul had a further thought. Faced with a
depraved and desperate city, he saw that if God could
bring about a miraculous change in the people and
spiritual climate of Corinth, he could do it anywhere—absolutely anywhere! So there was nothing
to lose. If ever there was a test case for establishing
that God has the power and ability to deal with
gigantic problems—this was it.

So with his eyes firmly fixed on Jesus, the 'author
and perfecter' of his faith, he cherished the challenge
of bringing the kingdom of God to Corinth. One
lesson Paul had already learned—a lesson that we,
too, would do well to remember—was to assess all
new situations from God's perspective rather than his
own. Corinth may have been daunting in Paul's eyes,
but it certainly was not a problem to God and Paul
was confident in his God. He was fully persuaded
that God could use him to overcome all the many
giants that were there, and he knew that those who
were with him in the spiritual realm far outshone
those who were against him.

In fact, Paul had discovered that great fact of all
facts: God is not only the King of kings; he's the Giant
of giants, the one who specialises in pulling down

strongholds and defeating the enemy. Therefore, as this Giant of giants had called him there and was committed to his success in bringing the kingdom to that place, the giants of Corinth had better watch out!

Indeed, within eighteen months Paul had pioneered and established an amazing church which was winning many of the people away from their hellish backgrounds. God had broken through! No one and nothing could come against him. Paul couldn't have agreed more with David when he declared in Psalm 56:9, 'One thing I know: that God is for me.' And in his letter to the Romans, Paul goes a step further when he states, 'And if God is for us, who can be against us?' (Rom 8:31). Not even the giants of Corinth.

There's no place like Corinth

My ministry has caused me to travel to many, many places and I have yet to go to a place that compares with Corinth then. So I am absolutely convinced that if God did it in Corinth, then there is no place on earth that is too hard for him today. No situation or circumstance is so far gone that he cannot change it. He declares in Jeremiah 32:27, 'Behold I am the Lord . . . Is there anything too hard for me?'

However, not everyone agrees, it seems! One of the things that never ceases to astound me is how many unbelieving believers I come across as I preach up and down the country. Many times I've heard a pastor, elder, deacon or church member say something like this: 'This is a real tough area, you know. We've tried everything and nothing seems to work here. You see, brother, there is a long history of occultism in our town.'

Or, if it's not occultism, there's some sort of strong cult in the area, or a masonic lodge, or there are a number of sex shops that are having a bad influence, or there is a group of spiritualists praying against them. In some places people tell me that the area is just too affluent; in others they believe it's too poor. Or again, there's massive unemployment, or crime, or social deprivation. . . and so it goes on. Whatever it is, there always seems to be a reason why where they are is the hardest place on earth. I really do wish I had a pound for every time someone told me that where they work or live is the most God-forsaken and darkest place in town!

Unfortunately these unbelieving believers fail to realise that this is exactly what the devil wants us to believe. He wants to intimidate us into thinking that the job in hand is too big and well beyond us, and that there is too much resistance. He knows if he can get us to succumb to giant Negative, we are defeated before we start.

It really is time to become believing believers again and live in the truth of 1 John 4:4: 'We are of God . . .' and 'greater is he that is in us, than he that is in the world'. When the enemy presses in and the giants are waging war, remind yourself that if God could slay the giants and pull down the strongholds in Corinth then he can do it anywhere—and that includes where you are!

It is also important to realise that God has placed you where you are 'for such a time as this'. There is no doubt that God has given us the capacity and the wherewithal as a church, as leaders and as individuals to face the giants that oppose us. Whatever form they take, we can defeat these giants and win through with the work of God. Don't believe the lies of the devil— God can and will give you the victory. So don't shrink back from the task ahead; keep pressing on regardless. Lay hold of that which Christ Jesus has laid hold of you for—and go for it.

The taming of a giant called Eddie

Eddie was the last guy you'd ever think would become a Christian. He was a tall, strong, well-built bloke, with longish ginger hair and a beard—the type of person you would definitely want to have on your side if you ever ran into a bit of bother!

We all worked together in the factory; you know— the factory where they used to chant 'Go-li-ath'. (Now that was a place. I still believe to this day that you haven't really seen life unless you've worked on the factory floor.) And if ever there was a thorn in my side, Eddie Roberts was it! Out of all the people who worked there, he was the one who got to me the most (not that I let him know that but it probably showed anyway). He was a real 'Jack the lad'. To be honest with you, we had some great laughs, but when it came to the things of God he just didn't want to know. In fact, he was positively hostile and even aggressive whenever the subject came up. Invariably, he was the one who would start chanting 'Go-li-ath' and the one who constantly ridiculed my faith.

I remember vividly how he used to accuse me of swearing. He'd say, 'Call yourself a Christian? You just swore,' and I would reply, 'I didn't.' Then he would say, 'You did.' Then he would call over to the other workers and shout, 'Hey lads! Didn't Phil just swear?' And they would all say 'You did, Phil. We heard you.' I fell for it every time, and I'd think, 'Lord, I'm sorry. I must really be in a bad way; I don't even know I'm doing it.' This was a regular occurrence. It was only on my last day at work that one of the lads pulled me aside and said, 'Phil, you know all the times we accused you of swearing? Well, you never did. We were only trying to wind you up— and it always worked!'

The Bible says that the devil is the accuser of the brethren. He was accusing me of all sorts of things I'd never done; and he got me in such a spin, I started to believe it. Eddie really knew how to add to this pressure. Sometimes it felt like constant barracking right throughout the day. It nearly drove me round the bend. I'd go home at night absolutely deflated and totally demoralised. Often I would moan to God, 'Lord you've put me in the hardest, darkest, toughest place there is on planet earth. There I am, God, in the factory day in and day out, trying to live a righteous life and be a witness for you and I'm making no headway at all. In fact things are getting worse, and as for Eddie Roberts, Lord, he's a lost cause. It would take more than a miracle to get him saved.'

Sometimes I got mad with God for not backing me up, but it never impressed him. I could almost imagine God winking or raising his eyebrows at Gabriel and saying, 'Look at him, he's off again. If only he knew!' When the time came for me to leave the factory, all I could say was, 'Thank God for deliverance!' I could now put the whole episode behind me.

Many, many years later, when I'd become a minister of a thriving church in Leicestershire and was married with two children, Eddie Roberts was a million miles away from my thoughts. I was with the family at the Bognor Bible Week. It was a sunny Sunday afternoon and we decided to walk down the promenade. We walked towards the town, stopping to chat to old friends we knew who were also attending the Bible week; and then we'd wish each other God's blessing and mosey on down the promenade, enjoying the sea-front breeze, without a care in the world.

And then suddenly I was riveted to the spot. At first I thought I was imagining things. I thought my brain was playing tricks on me. But no, there it was again.

'Go-li-ath.'

I could feel rigor mortis setting in. I knew instantly who it was. I turned around slowly, painfully, to see the infamous, the one and only Eddie Roberts, right back from those factory days. There was no mistaking him. He had hardly changed at all, except that he seemed to be walking with a limp.

'Hello, Eddie,' I said. 'Fancy seeing you here after all this time. What brings you here?'

He pointed to the camp and said, 'I'm at the Bible week. It's great, isn't it?'

I couldn't believe my ears. 'What do you mean you're at the Bible week? You don't come to things like this!'

'I do now,' he said.

'Hold on a minute, Eddie, let's backtrack a little. Are you a Christian now?'

His face lit up as he said, 'I sure am.'

I said, 'Get away, you're having me on.' I thought to myself: if he is having me on, pastor or no pastor, Bible week or no Bible week, he's dead meat!

He went on to share his testimony with us. I couldn't believe I was talking to the same Eddie who worked in the factory all those years before. As he shared, I didn't know whether to laugh, cry, hug him or shout hallelujah at the top of my voice. I was so jubilant I felt like cartwheeling down the promenade.

Apparently what had happened was this: shortly after I'd finished working in the factory, the place had had to close due to a fire that burned the premises to the ground. Everyone who worked there was made redundant and found themselves out of work. A week later, Eddie was involved in a horrendous accident, where his car went out of control and careered into a tree. I did actually see the police photographs of the wreckage, and believe me it was a miracle in itself that Eddie even survived the accident. However, somehow he did. But it did cost him one of his legs. He was rushed into hospital where he was to spend the next two months.

It was while he was in hospital that a Christian nurse started to witness to Eddie and show him that he needed the love of Christ in his life. After coming out of hospital he kept in touch with the nurse, and one evening she took him to a Christian meeting. From all accounts it was one of those real pentecostal, fire-burning experiences. That night, back at home, Eddie decided to invite the Lord Jesus Christ to be his personal Lord and Saviour, and from that time on he was a different man. The old Eddie had gone and the new one had come and it was plain for all to see! As he was sharing his testimony with me I couldn't help thinking what he used to be like. He was hardly the same man. I couldn't help thinking how I used to complain to God about him.

'What are you doing now, Eddie?' I asked.

'Oh I'm helping to pioneer a new church on an estate in Stoke-on-Trent.'

God had done it again. He had proved that nothing, absolutely nothing, was too difficult for him! And, to cap it all, Eddie married the nurse who had led him to the Lord.

If God can do amazing work in Corinth, and a miraculous work in Eddie, then there is simply nowhere and no one too difficult for God. Whatever situation you find yourself in, whatever giants you face in life, remember that 'no weapon formed against you can prosper, and no word spoken against you can stand'. Keep looking to Jesus, 'for greater is he that is in you than he that is in the world'. Indeed, our God is not only the King of kings; he's the Giant of all giants!

4

A Job for the Weak

Choosing the right people for the job is never easy. Today, managing directors, personnel staff and employers go to the greatest lengths to ensure they get the right people in the key positions. No expense is spared in looking into an applicant's education, qualifications, experience, health, family background and a whole host of other things. References will be sought, and then there will be a series of cleverly designed, in-depth interviews to guarantee the right appointment. In the cut-throat business world of the 1990s, no one wants to take on a loser or a failure.

In fact, in the present climate no one even wants to hire someone who is classed as good but ordinary. Employers are looking for people who are outstanding in their particular field, totally committed and absolutely professional in their approach. They want that little bit extra that will give their company the edge over its competitors. Head-hunting is common practice, along with lucrative contracts and sky-high salaries to entice key personnel from rival companies. No price is too high to find the right person—even if it does mean throwing in a sweetener or two!

God's ways and choices are so very different. Have you ever noticed the kind of people whom God chooses and uses to overcome the giants of life and to bring about his purposes? Most of them would never even get shortlisted in today's world, never mind an interview. But God seems to specialise in taking on minorities, the weak, the insignificant and the plain old ordinary from everyday walks of life. A look at the people he chose and used in biblical times proves the point:

- Jacob was a liar and a cheat, nothing but a twister.
- Moses was a shepherd in exile and a murderer; he was anything but articulate and was a superb maker of excuses.
- Gideon was a farmer and a part-time baker.
- Jephthah was the son of a prostitute.
- Hannah was a housewife.
- David was a shepherd boy and the last born of the family; he was sometimes uncontrollably fearful and always lonely.
- Ezra was a scribe.
- Esther was an orphan.
- Mary was a peasant girl.
- Matthew was a despised tax-collector.
- Thomas was a doubter.
- Luke was a family doctor.
- At least four of Jesus' disciples were fishermen.
- Paul started off as a tentmaker and an enemy of God's people; trouble seemed to follow him everywhere he went.

And so the list could go on and on.

You must admit, if you put all these qualities together they would hardly make the 'A' team today. Nevertheless, God believed in these people and hand-picked them to establish his purposes, overcoming gigantic opposition. I really do find it most encouraging, because if God could use these people then we're all in with a chance.

Jesus' team

In particular, the list above also shows that the team Jesus chose to work with left a lot to be desired. They were hardly the slick, qualified, gifted, professional, entrepreneurial executives that today's business world would have employed to challenge and change the world. Indeed, if Jesus had sought a 'professional' opinion, the final report might have read something like this.

From: Jordan Management Consultants Limited
Jerusalem

To: Jesus of Nazareth,
Son of Joseph,
The Carpenter's Shop,
Nazareth.

Dear Sir,

Please find herewith our professional consultation with regard to the team you are considering to spearhead your new enterprise.

It is our opinion that the men you are considering for management within your new organisation lack the background and the educational and vocational aptitude for the type of enterprise you are undertaking. They have very few formal qualifications and they certainly lack the team concept.

Personal profiles:

Simon Peter: highly strung and most unstable. He is given to emotional outbursts and fits of temper.

Andrew: shows no qualities of leadership or personnel management. He is happy to take a back seat and allows his brother to do his talking for him. (Having said that Peter tends to talk for everybody.)

James and John, the two brothers: these people place personal interest and ambition above company loyalty.

Thomas: demonstrates a questioning attitude that would tend to undermine morale. He doesn't like committing himself too quickly. In fact, the type of caution and questioning he does display could well lead to discouragement among your marketing force.

Matthew: having run the necessary data through our computer we feel it is our duty to inform you that this person has been blacklisted by the Greater Galilean Better Business Bureau. On further investigation we found that the business world tends to be extremely suspicious of all his professional dealings.

James and **Thaddeus**: reference information also shows that James, the son of Alphaeus, and Thaddeus have radical leanings, and in their personal assessments both registered high on the manic depressive scale.

Philip, Bartholomew and **Simon the Canaanite**: of these three candidates, we have been able to find out very little. This suggests that they may well have been unemployed and of no fixed abode. We hardly need remind you that taking on vagrants is almost always disastrous.

Judas Iscariot: this candidate, however, shows great potential. He is a man of ability and resourcefulness, has keen business acumen, and has many contacts in the highest places. He is highly motivated and exercises excellent entrepreneurial skills. We recommend that you appoint him as your organisation's controller, and your right hand man and personal assistant. We believe your organisation would prosper in his capable hands as he has drive and great initiative.

In conclusion, our research would suggest that all your team members, apart from Judas, are poorly qualified and ill-suited to spearhead such an organisation as yours. We have many other individuals on our books, in particular some extremely devout Pharisees, who might be more suitable. Perhaps we can help you? If so, please do not hesitate to get in touch.

We wish you every success in your new venture.

The Directors

It really does take some mental somersaults to understand why Jesus chose these people in the first place, but he did. This was the raw material he opted to work with. Instead of the many talented professional people he doubtless could have chosen, he chose a right motley crew. Jesus was obviously looking very keenly at qualities other than 'achievement potential'.

Now if you or I had been Jesus, would we have left the future of the whole church in the hands of this bunch? I'm pretty sure I wouldn't. But we'd have been wrong, as history has proved. So what criteria does God use in his selection process—a process which, at face value, seems totally beyond all human comprehension?

God chooses a shepherd king

A good place to begin is David's anointing as the king of Israel in the Old Testament (1 Sam 16:1–13). On that particular day in Bethlehem, no one would have given the boy David a hope of becoming anything more than a shepherd in his lifetime, let alone a king. For a start, he was up against his seven mega-talented elder brothers, so he hadn't the slightest expectation of even being considered for the position. He was the baby of the family—the mere lad who looked after the sheep. In comparison with him, his brothers were high-powered, attractive businessmen with their heads screwed on the right way, going about life and holding a real contempt and a total disregard for David. One of them, Eliab, greeted David quite scathingly and sarcastically when the latter appeared and was prepared to do battle with the Philistine giant, Goliath.

David's story begins when God sends Samuel, the prophet, to seek out and anoint the one who was to reign over Israel in Saul's place. Now where do you start looking if you want to fill the post of monarch? It's not every day you're asked to employ a king, and you can hardly advertise it in the Situations Vacant column!

The Lord told Samuel to go to Bethlehem and find a man called Jesse, for God had designated one of his sons to be the new king. When Samuel met up with Jesse and shared what God had said, you can imagine Jesse's excitement. This meant one of his sons would hold the highest position in the land and reign over the whole of Israel. Not only that, like 'the Queen Mum' Jesse was about to become 'the King Dad'!

Jesse naturally thought that Eliab, the eldest son, was the obvious choice. This tall, handsome, strong-looking, outstandingly gifted man fitted the bill to a 't'. If anyone held the required credentials and looked the part, it was Eliab. Samuel took one look at him and thought to himself 'Eureka! Look no further, Sam!

Surely this is the one!' But to Samuel's surprise, the Lord said, 'No, I have refused him. This is not the one.' God told Samuel not to be impressed by looks, height, or stature. 'For the Lord does not see as man sees; for man looks at the outward appearance, but the Lord looks at the heart . . .' (1 Sam 16:7).

God knows that we often overlook individuals who don't possess certain physical characteristics. But just as we can't judge a book by its cover, appearance never reveals what a person is really like. King Saul, David's predecessor, was literally head and shoulders above the rest when it came to stature. But his leadership abilities, his authority and his character did not, unfortunately, match up. There was simply no longer anything of the anointing of God on him.

When Eliab was rejected, Jesse then called six other sons to pass before Samuel, but Samuel declared that the Lord had not chosen any of them. Jesse must have felt it was all slipping away. He just couldn't understand it. If ever there was an array of the most brilliant and finest men in all the land—this was it. These seven sons were the most magnificent specimens of humanity. The crème de la crème, head and shoulders above the rest, the original 'magnificent seven'!

But God's approach to choosing a person is diametrically opposed to all this. God looks for a different type of material altogether. He looks at the heart, motives and intentions of a person, and physical perfection is always irrelevant to him. It is simply not in his criteria of choice at all. Alan Redpath, in his book, *The Making of a Man of God*, says this:

To educate and refine the flesh so that it becomes profitable in his service is never God's plan. He insists on the sentence of death upon everything that you and I are in ourselves. All that we are, apart from what we are given by his grace at the moment of our regeneration, is sentenced to God's judgement, no matter how intellectual or proud or clever or good we may be. There is only one place for all that is self—on Calvary.

In reality, God places no confidence in the flesh and neither should we.

'Are there any other sons?' Samuel asked.

Jesse replied, 'Yes, there is one, but he's the youngest and he just looks after the sheep.'

Now it's clear by the language Jesse uses that he doesn't think David is even worth considering. The phrase 'the youngest' suggests that David was the least in his father's estimation, the runt of the family so to speak—so inferior, indeed, that it was unnecessary to bother fetching him from the hillside in the first place.

Samuel says he will not rest until he's seen him and insists that he is sent for without delay. David is duly brought before the prophet and straight away God speaks to Samuel's spirit and says, 'This is the one. Arise and anoint him.' This is exactly what Samuel does, in full view of the rest of the family. No one could believe it at first, but it was true. God had chosen to use the most unlikely character in all Israel to become the next king.

Through our God we shall do valiantly

From the time of David's initial anointing on that dramatic day in Bethlehem, the Spirit of God came upon him in great power and used him to accomplish many significant things throughout his lifetime. But it wasn't all plain sailing. It often meant facing severe opposition, engaging in many hard battles, and challenging and overcoming many a determined giant.

The extent of David's victories is particularly noteworthy. If you were to plot on a map the places where he engaged in battle and defeated the various enemies who came against God's people, you would make a fascinating discovery. You would find that David's victory was absolutely complete. Powerful enemies surrounded Israel on every side and David in God defeated them all: the Philistines, who lived to the west; the Moabites, who lived further east; the Syrians, who came from the north and the north east; and the people of Edom, who inhabited the territory to the south and south east. For David, it was literally a case of victory in the north, south, east and west—victory on all sides, in all areas.

The thing is, David always moved in the power of God and under his clear direction. It was God who gave him the strategies, wisdom, confidence and wherewithal to win through against the greatest odds and the most unrelenting opposition: 'The Lord gave victory to David everywhere he went.' He overcame the champion, Goliath; he became king; he built up and led an army; and with his leadership he brought triumph after triumph demolishing every conceivable adversary. These achievements are considerable in their own right, but there is more . . .!

In the New Testament, Matthew 1 and Revelation 22:16 tell us that David had a part to play in God's wonderful plan to bring into this world the King of glory, Jesus, the Saviour; therefore David even had a part to play in the ultimate revelation of God's amazing love for humankind.

Now who would have believed all this of David—the one who was as good as written off by his own father? This was the one whom no one had any hopes for, or gave a prayer for. This was the one who was described as 'the youngest', and 'the lad'. This was the one who even wrestled in himself at times about his own value, usefulness and self-worth: 'I am a worm and not a man . . .' he wrote in Psalm 22:6. Yet regardless of all this, God still believed in him and chose to use him in a tremendous way to accomplish his glorious plans.

David isn't the only one to have felt inadequate over the years. Feelings of inferiority, insignificance, unimportance and utter worthlessness are major giants that have set out to destroy all types of talented and gifted people. Sadly, they have stopped many reaching their rightful position and fullest potential in God.

But God obviously looked on David and viewed him quite differently from the way other people saw him and indeed David sometimes saw himself. In God's eyes David was unique—as we are, too. The wonderful thing is that God sees us all in a different light. He sees us as winners even when we feel like, and look like, and are treated like, losers. Like David, we are choice servants and nothing less than world beaters and giant-killers!

Another strange choice

Someone else in the Old Testament who had a very low opinion of himself was Gideon. He was another one of 'God's strange choices', and we first hear of him as a farmer on his parents' farm in a place called Ophrah. God saw Gideon, too, in a totally different light from how Gideon saw himself. Judges 6 is where we pick up the story.

A little background and a lost opportunity

When Gideon came on the scene, the children of Israel had hopelessly and completely gone off the rails (once again!) and they'd started worshipping other gods. In doing so, the provision and protection of the Lord had been removed from them and it wasn't long before the Midianites were attacking Israel and running amok!

Now the Midianites were a desert people and Genesis 25:1–2 informs us that they were descendants of Abraham's second wife. Apparently, they were always at loggerheads with the Israelites, but the Israelites only had themselves to blame: many years earlier, while still wandering around in the wilderness, Israel had fought the Midianites and had had the opportunity of completely destroying them (Num 31:1–20). But they'd failed to do so, and the Midianites were now re-established and stronger than ever. By Gideon's time, Judges 6:5 tells us that their army was as innumerable as a swarm of locusts. They had a vast infantry, a host of camels, and incredible artillery. They really were a military force to be reckoned with. How the Israelites must have wished they had blown them away when they'd had the chance all those years earlier. The Midianites were making them pay for it.

As an aside, it's worth remembering that giants are often content to go incognito and lurk in the wings for a while as they regroup and re-establish themselves.

It's at such times that they build up strength, waiting for your spiritual defences to drop. They then make a comeback when the opportunity is right, just as the Midianites did, causing maximum hurt, devastation and chaos. That's why it's important to deal with a problem thoroughly and defeat it once and for all in the first place. David obviously realised this when he fought Goliath. You will recall that not only did he slay the giant but he went on to sever his ugly head as well. No way was David going to allow this giant to resurrect itself, make a comeback and fight another day. David made sure that this one was dealt with once and for all!

Now the Midianites were particularly ruthless and cruel in their attack this time. They had forced many of the Israelites to flee to the mountains for cover, where they hid, living in caves. The Midianites then ransacked the land, destroying all the crops and plundering all the animals and valuables. The war was in its seventh year and it was clear that the Israelites were losing. Having been stripped of everything they possessed, feeling totally demoralised, and being close to defeat, they decided to turn back to the Lord, pleading for divine intervention.

Wheat in the winepress

For Gideon, as for many others, it was a case of survival. He and his family were in hiding and he only had two aims—to protect his family and to provide for it. This in itself was no easy task in light of the continual onslaught and devastating crop destruction and pillage, but as a farmer Gideon would have been a little better off than some of the other Israelites because he would have had an amount of wheat in reserve to fall back on.

One day Gideon was threshing some wheat in the most unlikely place for a person to thresh wheat: his winepress. In threshing, the wheat grains were separated from the chaff, the worthless outer shell, by the wind, and normally therefore this was done out on the hillside. However, there was no way Gideon was going to risk being out in the open where he would become a prime target for the enemy. So he threshed his wheat in the winepress, and who could blame him? The winepress was a pit that was probably out of sight and it would be the last place anyone would look for a farmer's crops—or indeed a farmer, for that matter. Of course, there was no wind in the winepress to blow the chaff away but at the end of the day Gideon figured that bread with a bit of chaff in it was far better than being slaughtered and being found 'brown bread' (dead)! This was no time for heroics.

A warrior and a winner

So here was Gideon, working in this make-do threshing place, when he suddenly had the shock of his life. The angel of the Lord appeared next to him. You can imagine Gideon being totally taken aback; wouldn't you have been?

What is even more intriguing and captivating to me is how the angel of the Lord (who I believe was the Lord Jesus himself) greeted him. First of all, the angel declared that the Lord was with Gideon. Then he proceeded to address him as, wait for it, 'a mighty man of valour', 'a mighty warrior', 'a valiant warrior', or 'a mighty soldier', depending on which particular version of the Bible you use. This was some salutation for a man who found himself power-less, afraid and in hiding. Gideon must have thought the angel had made a major mistake, getting him mixed up with someone else. He must have got the wrong man. He had never been mistaken for 'a mighty warrior' in his life before! However, the angel hadn't got it wrong; Gideon was the person he was after.

Although Gideon could only see himself as a downbeat type of guy who was no one in particular, just totally insignificant and a born loser, God saw him from a completely different perspective. God saw him as a champion; a leader; a warrior; a winner!

If this was difficult enough to take in, worse was to come. The angel then told Gideon that God had chosen him to be the one to bring about Israel's deliverance from the hand of the Midianites. Gideon couldn't believe it and his low self-worth and inabil-ity began to surface. He said, 'How can I save Israel? My family is the least in Manasseh, and I am the youngest and the least thought of in my entire family.'

Just like David, Gideon never in a million years expected to be the one whom God would choose to defeat the enemy. Almost the whole of Israel was more capable than he was. He thought that the children of Israel would never even give him a second look, let alone endorse him as the captain of their army. But he was wrong, for the hand of God was on him. What Gideon had done was to make the common mistake of believing that his own inabilities, limitations and inadequacies would prevent God from ever wanting to use him; but he was wrong.

If you happen to be someone who thinks like this, let me encourage you: God does want to use us in spite of all our limitations and weaknesses. In choosing a person, one thing God doesn't look for is ability. What would the omnipotent creator of heaven and earth want with our mingy little abilities, no matter how great they might appear to us? No, as the cliché goes, it is not our *ability* that God is after, but our *availability*. And like all clichés, it has a lot of truth in it. God is looking for men and women who are available to do what he says and go where he leads. There are many people who are naturally multi-gifted and multi-talented whom God never uses because they never make themselves available for what he wants them to do at the time he wants them to do it.

Gideon was neither multi-gifted nor multi-talented, but he did make himself available to the will of God. The rest, as they say, is history. God used Gideon to lead the children of Israel into a tremendous victory over the mighty Midianite army, with an army just 300 strong, and without any of them engaging in any physical combat whatsoever.

Read about it for yourself in Judges 6 and 7. You will find it a real encouragement and a great source of blessing, especially if you are facing a situation you think is too big for you to handle. It will show you that there is nothing too big for God. It will also show you that he uses the most unlikely people to achieve victory in seemingly impossible circumstances.

Scripture is full of 'ordinary' people (or, as with David and Gideon, less than ordinary people) whom

God chose to overcome enormous opposition and accomplish most extraordinary things. Paul sums it up in 1 Corinthians 1:27 when he says, 'God has chosen the foolish things of the world to put to shame the wise, and God has chosen the weak things of the world to put to shame the things which are mighty.' It might seem strange to us, but God really does delight in using these things.

Hall of faith

As for David and Gideon, they are both mentioned in the great hall of faith recorded in Hebrews 11:32–34. We are left in no doubt that David, Gideon and the others did their mighty deeds and received what was promised, accomplishing what they did, not through their own ability but through faith. God responded to their availability, took their weaknesses and transformed them into great strengths with which to bring down giants. It is no different today where we are concerned.

A shoe clerk makes his mark

The whole of this chapter has focused on the apparent weakness of the people in the Bible whom God chose to do his work. The point is, it's still the same today. Let's look at the following few examples.

Edward Kimbell was a young Christian man who lived in Chicago, earning his living as a shoe clerk. He wasn't necessarily mega-talented or multi-gifted. In fact he was just an inexperienced, ordinary type of guy. As a sideline, however, he developed a real gift for children's work and felt it right to become a Sunday school teacher in his local church.

As a result, he began to spend hours of his free time visiting and meeting the young street urchins in Chicago's inner city. His desire was simply to tell them about Jesus and invite them to his Sunday school, and in 1858, because of this, a young boy by the name of Dwight Moody decided to commit himself to Jesus Christ. D. L. Moody grew up to be a preacher. Twenty-one years later, in 1879, Moody won someone else to the Lord—a young person by the name of F. B. Meyer who also grew up to be a preacher. Some time later, Meyer won a young person to the Lord by the name of Billy Sunday.

The chain of inspiration continued. Billy was a great athlete and in time he became a great evangelist. It was not long before Billy was invited to hold some evangelistic meetings in Charlotte, North Carolina. These revival meetings were so successful that the evangelist Mordecai Hamm was invited to conduct a follow-up mission. And when Hamm preached, another teenager gave his life to the Lord Jesus Christ, and this most recent convert was no less than Billy Graham himself.

Today, Billy Graham has become the most well-known evangelist in the world and has preached to more people than anybody else, bringing untold millions to the Lord Jesus Christ. Edward Kimbell in his lifetime may never have realised the repercussions of what God did indirectly through him. This shoe clerk simply made himself available to work in a Sunday school in Chicago. But that availability is still having its effect today.

Now you may not be a D. L. Moody, or a Billy

Sunday or a Billy Graham, but if you make yourself totally available to God, who knows what he will do through you? One thing is for sure: you are unique and you're beloved of God. The rest is up to you!

5

Giant Negative: (i) It's Personal

It was time to move to our third church. Before we even arrived, however, I began to wonder what I'd let myself in for because it seemed I may have been jumping out of the frying pan into the fire. You see, two previous ministers of the church contacted me quite independently to say they'd heard where I was going and seriously suggested that I reconsider my decision. Both of them had been the sad casualties of a more than difficult church. It didn't take a huge leap of the imagination for me to wonder whether I, with my own past experience, was exactly the right person for 'a difficult church'.

The church had got itself a bit of a bad reputation over the years. It had always appeared to struggle, with a number of domineering people who had become like a cork in a bottle, stopping the contents going anywhere. Of course, the church had had some great pastors as well as some not-so-great ones, but for one reason or another almost all of them had left either demoralised or ill, and there were all sorts of internal wrangles. Some had even suffered heart attacks, strokes, or breakdowns during their stay, and more than one had buckled under the strain of being subtly told that they were surplus to requirements and had outstayed their welcome.

But God can and does change things, including churches. That's the whole message of resurrection. He challenged and changed me. And gradually over the years he was to change this church. The first significant breakthrough came when three elders of the church went away and repented before God of the past (although interestingly, not one of them had been around at the beginning). Nevertheless, the bad spirit of giant Negative that had been crippling the church for years still needed some more tough handling for the enemy's stronghold to be completely broken.

The upward movement really took hold with a former pastor, who to my mind had a very successful ministry. Indeed, he had a track record of going into difficult situations and sorting them out. He had a gift of getting to grips with the real issues and people who were stopping a move of God. I believe this is exactly why he was sent to this particular church. He did a superb job of tackling and dealing with those who domineered and controlled. It took him all of the six years he was there but there was a price to pay—a heart attack and a stroke—but he left the job well done; it now had a right spirit about the place, and it was prepared for growth.

This man was also able to get the church on a sound financial footing for the first time in its history. Indeed, if its former finances were anything to go by, it was amazing that it hadn't folded years before. Of course, some people may think that considering its attitude and bad reputation, it wouldn't have been a bad thing if it had closed down. But at the end of the day, God knows what he is doing and he knows the end from the beginning. He had planned that there would be a time when the church would become significant and blossom into something beautiful, even if it was nearly forty years after its birth. We should never be too quick to write a place off. Who knows what God has in store for it, even if it is a few years down the road?

When we arrived there was a buzz of excitement about the place and it was ready to go. We couldn't have received a better welcome, and we went on to have seven-and-a-half fantastic years there. We saw God do some truly amazing things and we experienced some phenomenal growth. By that time, there were three full-time paid staff, a part-time church worker and an almost-full-time administrator. The church had a great worship band, a talented drama team, an excellent evangelistic team, and an extremely successful luncheon club which made inroads into the local community.

The church also became involved in birthing a number of other churches. It literally went from being a difficult church to a dynamic church, having to hold four services every Sunday to accommodate the volume and diversity of people who were attending. It was an exciting place to be. If I hadn't been the pastor, it's exactly the type of church I would have joined. It was my type of place and they were my type of people. Some places are difficult to leave and this was one of them. When we did leave, we felt truly bereft and we owe a lot to our time there.

Many people have asked me what it was that caused the church to grow. I have sat down for hours pondering over this one, and even now I find it difficult to give a definitive answer, although I am sure it was an accumulation of things. I guess the apostle Paul sums it up in 1 Corinthians 3:6–8 when he says, 'I planted, Apollos watered, but God gave the increase.' Of course, there were many difficulties and oppositions to overcome and many giants to slay, but God in his mercy broke through and established a thriving and significant work in that small town.

A negative start

Now when we first arrived we were determined to prove God and let nothing and no one stand in the way of what he wanted to do. But we had only been there a couple of days when someone pulled me aside and said, 'Pastor, can I have a private word in your ear? You will appreciate that I've been around a long time, almost from the very beginning. I've seen pastors come and I've seen pastors go. I've seen good times here and I've seen bad times. So do you mind if I give you a couple of tips?'

Eager to learn I replied, 'Of course, fire away.'

'Firstly,' he said, 'I think it is best if you don't implement too much change. You see we like it the way it is—small and cosy. Secondly, whatever you do, never have a meeting on a Saturday night. They're a dead loss. We've tried them over the years and they've never worked and they never will, mark my words. So do yourself a favour and don't waste your time. You see, Pastor, God doesn't seem to work on Saturday nights round here.'

Talk about red rag to a bull. Straight away I felt the rebel rising within! From that moment on, everything within me wanted to arrange a Saturday night meeting. I was so cussed I was determined to do it just to prove that God was not in the habit of having Saturdays off!

Tradition

The giant of Tradition in the local church can be a massive giant to overcome. You see, people who have been in a place for a long time constantly feed Tradition with fodder that says 'We have always done it this way before' all over the packet. But it is so important never to allow any moribund church tradition to influence or dictate the way ministry and outreach should go.

As Christmas was approaching, I naturally thought this was the ideal opportunity to make the point. I decided to hold 'ye olde-fashioned, traditional, Saturday night carol service' as well as the usual Sunday night one. Having done everything I could to inspire and motivate the people in the church about this special outreach night, we set to prayer. The church began to get excited—that is, apart from a few fully paid-up members of the 'Negative Opposition Party' who were led by guess who. That's right, the guy who took me aside for the private word. (By the way, they tell me there is a branch of the NOP in every church.)

We designed a simple Christmas card wishing the people of the town a Happy Christmas and a Blessed New Year, and inviting them to our special Saturday night carol service. It was hard work delivering the 17,500 cards we had printed but there was no alternative—no way could we afford to pay to have them delivered. There was nothing for it except to rely on

Shank's pony! In the build-up to Christmas I constantly encouraged my congregation to bring a friend
and come early because the place would be absolutely
chock-a-block, and we were going to see God at work;
it would be a watershed in the life and growth of the
church. I must confess, when you come out with faith
statements like this it doesn't half activate your
prayer life in a certain direction!

The big day came and there was no need to worry.
God blessed in a mighty way. As usual, he was so
faithful and so gracious in his dealings with us. The
church was literally wall-to-wall with people. Every
seat in the house was filled and in many cases there
were two to a seat. There were people sitting on the
floor, down the aisles, in the foyer. There were bodies
everywhere. It was uncomfortable. It was electric. It
was amazing.

A number of people at that meeting also put their
trust in the Lord Jesus Christ for the first time and
without question the church was the better for holding that Saturday night service because we definitely
grew through it. So who says God doesn't work on
Saturday nights? And it was all repeated on the following night as well! I am pleased to say this was the
first of many regular and successful Saturday evening
programmes. When we dare to step out for God he
always honours our faith.

The point I am making here is an important one.
Don't let the giant Negative (with Tradition frequently tagging along behind it) determine the
way ahead, no matter how long it's been around
and no matter how many pastors it's seen bite the
dust.

Favourite sayings of giant Negative

The growth and development of any local church, personal ministry, great project, vision or business venture, is often thwarted and held back through negative thinking. Too many times giant Negative wins the day. Giant Negative is extremely vocal and always makes itself known in one way or another. It doesn't matter what you know God is telling you to do or in what direction he is clearly leading you, there is always someone who comes up with a multitude of reasons why it can't be done.

- We've tried it before. (It didn't work.)
- We can't afford it.
- Who's going to do it? (Not me.)
- We haven't got the time.
- We mustn't bite off more than we can chew.
- It's too different.
- We've never done it like this before.
- It's worldly.
- The people won't like it.
- I'm against it.
- We like it the way it is.
- It will never work.
- God doesn't work around here on a Saturday/ Monday/in August/ever.

These are all favourite sayings of giant Negative. In church life, two of the most used phrases are, 'The previous pastor wouldn't have done it this way,' and, 'It wasn't like this in the good old days.' In fact the list is endless. There are always hundreds of negatives.

Now giant Negative, like most giants, is clever.

Don't be taken in by its crafty, manipulative ways. It isn't always aggressive and up front, shouting the odds; sometimes it is quietly working in the background causing a disquiet and an undercurrent which you can never seem to put your finger on. It can even be gentle, reasonable and persuasive. In fact, it doesn't mind what method it uses to halt your progress as long as it does. One thing you can be sure of, though, is that it will consistently say the same old thing—'It can't be done'—even if it does wrap the arguments up nicely in reason and tie them with a pretty bow of logic!

A Negative Opposition Party

Nehemiah in the Old Testament had a great vision of rebuilding the walls of Jerusalem. He even gained the king's approval and support. In fact, the king placed before him a wide open door and prepared the way for him to fulfil the task that God had given him to do. Nehemiah went on to motivate and inspire a vast number of people, but it wasn't long before Sanballat and Tobiah came on the scene.

It was through these two men that giant Negative manifested itself and sprang into action. Sanballat and Tobiah poured cold water on Nehemiah's vision right from the outset (Neh 2:19). Nehemiah wasn't deterred, but neither were Sanballat and Tobiah who fervently continued in their ridicule and opposition (Neh 4:1–3). You see, giant Negative is always persistent and is never easily put off. It will push you to the limit until it can push you no more. Sanballat and Tobiah tried every tactic to frustrate the work of God—downright opposition, ridicule, lies, aggression, and scheming and plotting the downfall of Nehemiah. Of course, they also lobbied and rallied all the other negative people and formed the 'Negative Opposition Party'.

Nothing has changed today. You still find some folk who love to be cynical and antagonistic, placing themselves firmly in the opposition corner. Have you ever noticed how negative folk always manage to find each other and club together? In Eric Berne's famous book, *Games People Play*, the game called 'Ain't it Awful?' describes a script that some people literally live by all their lives—basically, all the things they ever think or say boil down to 'Ain't it awful?' How sad! And they like nothing more than to feed off each other's so-called disasters.

What's more, even people who don't normally get on together will join ranks if it suits them to oppose you. Giant Negative has a special interest in getting such like-minded people introduced to each other, for together they gossip all manner of things into being. It was most probably Negative that got Sanballat and Tobiah together in the first place.

Still, as we said before, it is God's business to accomplish great things through ordinary people in the midst of the most fervent ridicule and opposition. Despite all the resistance of Sanballat and Tobiah, the walls of Jerusalem were rebuilt in record time—just over fifty days. Even Israel's enemies had to admit that God was with these builders in a special way. Once again, in God an almost impossible task was accomplished.

The world is full of modern-day Sanballats and Tobiahs and unfortunately even the church seems to have its fair share of fully paid-up NOP members. The

answer is to rise above it all, whether it comes from
without or within. Pray your way through it and keep
standing on the promises of God. Decide that every
negative and set-back will make you that little bit
more determined.

The late great comedian Les Dawson had the right
kind of attitude when it came to dealing with the
negatives of life. During an interview he was asked
to what or to whom he owed his success. He replied,
'I would like to thank all those people who over the
years didn't believe in me for one reason or another.
Thank you so very much for all you have done in
helping me forge the sword of my determination.'
Now that's the spirit!

A word of advice about advice

As a believing believer you are bound to run into
your fair share of pessimists. Now don't get me
wrong, you can't reject experienced advice outright.
The doubts of the mind need to be investigated, and
you must give adverse advice the appropriate weight
in coming to a decision otherwise giant Pride will be
sitting there laughing its head off. It is quite right to
investigate, to take time to find the cause, source and
reasoning of contrary opinions.

But you can't allow other people's advice to over-
whelm your inner feelings so much that you also
doubt in your heart. Instead, use the advice and any
negative feedback to go back to God and the Scriptures, and look deeply into the heart of your venture
with a clear, critical eye. If, having sought God, you
feel there is an element of truth in what is being said,
then show giant Pride the door and be sensible

enough to change your stance. However, if such investigation convinces you that the 'experts' are in error, then to pot with their torpedoes—go full speed ahead!

The power of positive thought

The problem with doubts of the heart is that we so often feed them ourselves by meditating upon them. And when we feed them, they grow out of all proportion and become giants that neutralise all our efforts. But if we starve them of negative thought, they will quickly die of malnutrition. So don't entertain them. The thing you should be feeding is your faith. Jude 20 tells us we should be building ourselves up in the most holy faith.

It's a bit like having two wavelengths on the radio. Tune in to the negative wavelengths and you'll be in confusion, doubt and fear. If you want to succeed and get ahead, tune in to the positive wavelengths and the good ideas. Feed your positive thoughts with faith, fill your mind with the wonderful affirmations and the powerful promises from the word of God. Anyone who walks the journey of faith needs consistent spiritual nourishment. The reason why so many people fail is because they are spiritually undernourished, and they are not building themselves up in God. Not one of us can stop the negatives coming our way, but we all have the power to choose the wavelengths we tune in to.

Insulation and immunisation

There are a number of ways you can immunise yourself from the germs of personal negativity that so often grow into giants. They will help you to move forward, upward and onward in God.

1. Immunisation through the word

Go back to the word of God and find and underline all those verses and passages of Scripture that have given you courage, confidence and conviction. As you memorise these and let them sink deep into your spirit, you will find that when the negative forces attack they will bounce off you better. They might sting you for a couple of minutes but they will do you no real harm.

The word of God is still with power. Romans 10:17 tells us that 'faith comes by hearing, and hearing by the word of God'. Some of the modern versions of the Bible only use the word 'hearing' once in this verse. I have used the new Authorised version, where it mentions 'hearing' twice, because I feel it is a much more accurate rendering. You see, it is not as simple as picking up the Bible when things are not going according to plan, for a quick read to receive enough faith to sort things out. Too many people treat the Bible as if it were magical. Faith is only activated when the word of God is a part of our everyday life. Mountain-moving faith only comes by hearing and hearing and continually hearing the word of God. Make a quality decision to devote yourself to the word, making sure that you become an effectual doer and not just an ineffective hearer.

Then, when times are really hard, as a friend very usefully said to me once, 'You can still be faithful even if you can't feel your faith.' You can hang on in there. Because at the end of the day, it is 'the implanted word' of God active in our lives that will cause us to win through and effect change.

2. *Learn to channel your thoughts*

Our thought lives are always in need of fine-tuning. It is important to channel all our thoughts. Philippians 4:8 says, 'Whatever things are true, whatever things are noble, whatever things are just, whatever things are pure, whatever things are lovely, whatever things are of good report . . . think on these things.'

Stick the following questions on your office or kitchen door, and whenever something enters your head, ask yourself:

- Is it really true?
- Is it positive or negative?
- Is it good or evil?
- Is it productive or counter-productive?
- Is it constructive or destructive?
- Is it healthy or unhealthy?

If it is true, or noble, or just, or pure, or lovely, or positive, 'meditate on these things'. If it isn't, ignore it completely (giants simply hate being ignored); chuck it out.

3. *Feed your mind with positive influences*

Believe it or not you can choose many of the thoughts that come your way by selecting the right literature to read, listening to the right things that come your way and even by watching the right types of television programmes and films. Don't expose yourself unnecessarily to the negative influences. Make sure you guard your mind and heart. You can't feed on the world's giants and have God's word come out of your mouth in faith and power. It just won't work. What you give your attention to outside is what's going to be on the inside of you. 'Above all, guard your hearts.'

4. Guard your conversation

Be careful what you talk about. You will find that engaging in idle gossip and character assassination will affect your spirit and sap your faith. Have nothing whatever to do with it. The world is full of negatives and pessimists but you don't have to be one.

5. Mix with possibility thinkers

Choose as your closest friends and confidantes those who are spiritually dynamic—possibility thinkers who encourage others and build them up. As iron sharpens iron, one person sharpens another. Mix with people who will walk the way of faith with you. Of course, you will also spend your time as a Christian as Jesus did with the have-nots of this world and many of their lives will be full of negativity. But while you stay alongside them in compassion, do also allow positive-thinking people to aid God's power centre in your life.

6. Insulate yourself by developing your relationship with Jesus Christ

This is the beginning point as well as the end one. Your relationship with Christ is the most important thing in the world. What is it like? Are you growing in faith? Is your devotional life up to scratch? Having a strong relationship with God will keep the personal giant Negative at bay. At all times keep your eyes fixed on him for he is 'the author and perfecter of your faith'.

So there we have it. You don't have to be governed by the negatives in your own personal life. You can train yourself to think positively and move forward in God.

6

Giant Negative: (ii) It's Corporate

We may have ended the last chapter on a high, but believe me—the devil will always have another go. And if he can't get you to be negative via the personal route, he may try one of the cruellest routes of all—the corporate route.

I have seen this giant. I've seen it, glowering at me, with 'Corporate' faintly tattooed across its forehead. I've seen it and my heart has gone out to every dispossessed person, every refugee, every unemployed father and mother, every person who has ever fought for justice and who has ever come up against that grey, immovable, elephantine giant known as 'the system'. If you've seen it too, you'll know what I'm talking about because you too will have been up against it, sensing that every pore of its being seems designed to help anyone but you. It's nigh on impossible to find out where it begins and where it ends; in fact it has roots and branches in places you didn't even know existed. And it's one of the most sinister forces that can affect people's lives.

Corporate negativity is, in fact, just another facet of giant Negative. You can track it throughout history, clubbing its way under the guise of the 'powers that be'. Think of the millions of Africans shipped to slavery in the seventeenth and eighteenth centuries. The giant Corporate certainly carved up their lives good and proper. Think of the highland clearances in Scotland, when the landowners decided to 'clear' the hillsides of people 'because there were too many of them'! Think of the Jews, gassed by the Nazi system. Think of many refugees today, in countries the world over. Think of the thousands of prisoners known to Amnesty International whose cases are turned down by every appeal board open to them.

Think, too, of the homeless, the penniless, the mental patients let back into 'the community', the single parents, who so often get no further than the bureaucrats and the faceless word 'No'. Time and time again, it is the dispossessed who get it in the neck, to their own constant, drip-drip-drip disadvantage. It gets even worse because giant Corporate always courts giant Frustration and two-times with giant Disappointment. Together they wield a vile weapon—the supple, razor-sharp edge of the system that can grind people to the ground if they let it. When it really gets to them, it can tear their souls apart.

Keep your dreams

The first piece of good news is that when we hit the system, God is on our side. We don't *have* to be defeated by corporate negatives any more than we do by personal negatives. The secret is to keep our God-given dreams.

Take someone I once met called Jonathan Taylor. This wonderful guy had been born in 1967 with a certain amount of brain damage. Although he was fine mentally, he had a deformed right hand and wrist. Writing, shaking hands, holding and gripping were just not possible for Jonathan—not with that hand anyway. Of course, it made life difficult at times but he learned to live with his disability and just did everything with his other hand.

Jonathan battled his way through school, and the time inevitably came for him to consider his career possibilities. He knew exactly what he wanted to do, for his dream was to become a chef. However, on visiting the careers officer, he received nothing but discouragement. The careers officer doubted his academic ability to achieve the necessary qualifications to pursue such a career, and he was absolutely certain Jonathan wouldn't be able to cope physically with his disability. How could he carry hot pans of water and food around the kitchen without endangering himself and others who worked in the kitchen? How could he possibly slice and dice, cut and prepare with only one good hand? It was, apparently, impossible and he was strongly advised to forget it and go for something else.

All this did was make Jonathan more determined. He decided to apply for a place at the local catering college, determined in his heart to do it. He would just have to prove he could do all the things they said he couldn't do. After discussing things in detail, he persuaded the college to accept his application for the City and Guilds catering course. This was an achievement in itself and he was on his way. It was tough and he had to work twice as hard, both academically and practically, than some other students, but to his credit he stuck with it and by the end of the first year he'd passed the first two City and Guilds exams. There was only one more to go.

Then Jonathan suffered another setback. He was advised seriously to consider dropping out of the next part of the course. It was felt by the faculty of the college that it would be just too intense and frustrating for Jonathan. He had little choice; they were very persuasive and he took their advice.

However, the dream never left him. He still wanted more than anything to become a qualified chef. So a few years later, he successfully reapplied to another college to take the remaining part of the course and he finally became a fully qualified chef. What they said he couldn't do, by the grace of God he did. He proved himself to be nothing but an absolute winner. If he had failed to get the necessary qualifications to become a chef, he would still have been a winner. For anyone who tries and gives it their best shot is an absolute winner in God's eyes!

Jonathan Taylor is just one person who got negative advice from the system. It couldn't have been more wrong. It hadn't reckoned on the type of stuff this man was made of and it failed to see that 'greater was he that was in him'. You see, just because experts and professionals say you can't do something, it doesn't mean they're right. Of course, you have to keep to the law, but within that you can still determine in your heart that no one except God is going to set the boundaries of your life.

Lean not on your own understanding and keep going

Now you may be saying, 'My dreams are not enough,' and you'd be right! Your personal dreams are not enough. Dreams without God will never get you by.

The funny thing is, while the giant Corporate can be particularly ruthless and debilitating, in a strange way it really can help your cause because the system can be so inflexible that it utterly throws you back, not on your own resources but on God's. So the second piece of good news is this: the very best thing to do when you come up against the system is to keep trusting God, and keep faith in *his* ability to see you through—even if you can't see it. God will help you try another way, over and over and over again. If anything teaches us that it is he who has the power rather than human beings, then beating giant Corporate is it. Of course it is frustratingly painful, but God is with you and for you and all things can work together for good. God really can make a way when there is no way.

The horrors of the giant Corporate can also, however, be attacked on a third front. Now I'm not suggesting that it's easy, when you're really up against it, to do anything else other than stick close to God—but there is another practical step you can take.

Our own expectations

The third key point to remember in facing 'the system' is actually to *let go of what we expect of it*. For instance, because we expect the police to be honourable we are astounded when confronted by a dishonest police officer and may hold a grudge for months or years afterwards. But later, we find it is not the police that burden our soul, it's our grudge—our old enemy

giant Bitterness, no less. Equally, because we expect
the 'free and impartial' press not to twist the truth, we
get so upset when it does that we feel like never
trusting it again; understandably so. But unfortunately what is damaged in the process is not the
newspaper concerned; it is our ability to trust another
time.

Hope and heavenly expectation

Let's be absolutely clear about one thing. There's an
enormous difference between our heavenly expectations—our God-given hopes through the Holy
Spirit—and our expectations in this world. Our
hope in God is our profoundest and most wonderful
expectation, and one of which we may be certain. We
can 'hold on firmly to the hope we possess, because
we can trust God to keep his promise' (Heb 10:23).

Giant Expectation and unreality

Pinning our hopes on what the world has to offer is
totally different. In fact, it's crazy, because it's precisely this kind of expectation that fools us and lets us
down so badly. When it comes to the system, our
expectations can become so massive that we get
utterly confused by all manner of 'should's and
'shouldn't's. Before we know it, we have another
giant in our lives!

This would be bad enough, but the trouble is, giant
Expectation frequently tempts us to be out of touch
with reality as well. Of course, the devil just delights
in doing this. He will tell you that at the very least the
'powers that be' should pay you attention and oh-so-

deserved honour, fairness and respect into the bargain—the Nobel Prize for Wonderfulness, no less. When life turns out differently, the devil then tries to coax you to a slap-up meal served on a glittering platter by Resentment. But where, now, is reality? Instead of seeing what's real, all we see now are our inflated expectations. Reality itself has become unpleasant, and is often a nasty shock.

Now if Expectation gets in the way of the truth, it really is incredibly dangerous. If we listen to it, we will end up living in a world of make-believe and 'what should be'. Of course, the giant Corporate and giant Expectation know all this, and boy do they play on it! They even encourage us to have expectations about the sacred institutions of marriage and the family—what is expected of partners, children, parents, siblings and not least yourself.

So we simply have to let our worldly expectations go. We must see the devil in them and recognise that what he's doing is horribly negative. He's the absolute maestro of glamorous expectation, and just loves to whip us up into a romantic frenzy (with giants Expectation, Greed, Jealousy and Rivalry all dancing alongside). But if he wins, it'll be giant Disappointment that comes along to clean up afterwards.

Let me repeat: if we have the wrong expectations of the world, we really are doomed. We will become embittered, and lose sight of reality (and, more importantly, what is good about reality). In this context, we really must 'let go and let God'.

Is Christ before me?

It's a curious thing, but the problem of expectation is probably at its subtlest and most dispiriting in our faith. It is here that both giant Corporate and giant Expectation are at their most cunning, because so often Christians expect more.

As we saw in the last chapter, the personal giant Negative is already quite at home in some individuals in our churches. Unfortunately, the corporate giant Negative is very much at home here too. Along with giant Expectation, it frequently invites people to invest so much misplaced hope in serving on such-and-such a committee, or seeking a certain system of healing, or finding a new church, that, unless the individuals concerned are truly and prayerfully in line with God's purposes for them, negative disappointment and frustration are inevitable.

And it gets worse. Distinguishing giant Corporate actually becomes very difficult in churches because here this giant is often totally disguised, especially in those big, wealthy churches that wield a lot of political, bureaucratic and administrative muscle. Many in the leadership structures are unwilling to criticise their own power. They'd rather ignore it and pretend it isn't there. But it is. It's just another tentacle of another octopus-like system, as those on the receiving end know only too well.

Even ministry itself can have its frustrating and damaging expectations. Take church planting, for example. It sounds so romantic to go and plant a church with twenty new members. Expectations run high, but sometimes people fail to see reality. Consequently, they battle on with twenty members for years and years with nothing really happening, and sooner or later giants Disappointment and Frustration will descend—some more disenchanted souls to add to their long and far-reaching list! Of course, there's nothing wrong with church planting, but there's nothing romantic about it either. We really need to be called by God. Only in him can we truly hope. Outside him, we can't. We need to see through both the system and the institutional church, and pin our hopes on nothing more or less than the Lord himself.

Expectation versus forgiveness

What about the whole area of expectation versus forgiveness? Let us turn now to the inspiring wisdom in Jesus' own teaching. For instance, the Gospels tell us that Jesus instructed Peter to forgive not seven times, but seventy times seven. Let me ask you a question. Have you ever tried to forgive someone more than once for the same thing? The first time, of course, it's relatively easy—after all, you're just being a Christian: to forgive, to turn the other cheek and so on. But when the same person repeats the same offence against you a second time, it gets a little trickier— downright irritating in fact. The same customer makes the same racist remark about your ethnic background, or the same colleague cuts you dead in the street just like they did last week; and suddenly Expectation (with Disappointment, Frustration and Resentment lining up in the wings) sees its chance and steps right up to you, smirking, bright-eyed, and hoping for a foothold.

'You should expect better than this,' it remarks, as it lurks propped up against your front door. 'You made it clear last time that this dude has the wrong attitude. He should be sorry. He owes it to you. This can't go on!'

But it's only the second time. You steel yourself. 'Get thee behind me, Satan,' you say. 'This person obviously didn't hear my response the first time, so I'll let him off again. Besides, don't you know? I'm a Christian!'

However, the third time the same person does the same thing, you start getting genuinely hot under the collar. 'This really should have stopped by now,' you hear a voice saying; and, reluctantly, you're beginning to agree with the giant.

Now the offence being perpetrated against you is actually the same the third time as it was the first. But it's really beginning to get to you. By the fourth time it happens, Expectation has you frothing at the mouth with outraged indignation and frustration and by the seventh it's definitely all-out war!

But Jesus tells us to forgive seventy *times* seven, and he's not joking. This is mind-blowing! Your expectation is certainly that by now the offender should have been hung, drawn and quartered, and his or her every friend and family member should have been packed off to Siberia for life, if not longer! But no. What Jesus tells us is that if we have any hope of living for God in this life, we have to let it all go, to behave on the five hundredth occasion as if it were the first. Having expectations will only hang us up, he says, and the kingdom of God is just not like that. Instead we are asked to let go time after time after time—and yet at the same time to keep on trying for God.

You see, many Christians are giant-infested because they just refuse to let go and forgive. But Jesus tells us that dropping every single earthly expectation we have is the *only* way forward in order to have his kind of spiritual freedom; in order truly to live life in humble service to God. It is so simple, and yet it is a very tall order.

Back to the system

It is encouraging to know that Jesus also had the system to contend with. In fact, he made many remarks about the system. He told people not to get so worked up about what they should or shouldn't pay to Caesar, or so entangled with the rituals of the Jewish faith that they couldn't find God any more. The Sabbath was a major institution that people had expectations about, but here too Jesus cracked open the hypocrisy and expectation in the cause of the love of God when he healed the man with the withered hand on this apparently special day. Letting go the expectations of the system was just as much part of what Jesus was talking about. The great thing is, Christ himself has gone before us, as in everything, and shown us how to do it.

Jesus was there

The giant Corporate in the Bible, especially in the first century, was just as big for the early Christians as it is for many people today. If the system required you to carry a soldier's pack for a mile, you did so or you were punished. Everyone from beggars to Herod had to toe the Roman line. The synagogues too represented power and inflexibility with tier upon tier of tradition, and there were rigid rules about who did what and when and where. Dare to step out of line, and that system too would mete out its loveless discipline to every miserable offender.

In fact, given the circumstances, it is amazing that Jesus was only angry once in the Bible—at traders who used God's temple for profit. If it had been me, I would have been frustrated and angry at the system practically all day every day. Yet Jesus only had compassion for its victims, and he simply wouldn't harbour giant Corporate.

This is even more incredible when we remember that it was the system that actually took away Jesus' life on earth. The Pharisees, the Romans, Pilate, the Sanhedrin, the devil, the crowds at his trial, Judas, and even, briefly, his disciples—all were against him at some point. He knew what it was to be loved by no one but God, friendless, and crucified both by the 'powers that be' and by his own people in his own land. But despite the system, Jesus came through and so can you. It's why we can trust that his way really is the best way. He's been there first so that we can forge ahead in him. He knows the way. All we need do is follow.

No expectations?

Perhaps you think you are above all this; you are far too wise to have expectations of the system. It may be so. But one thing to remember is this: it's not always our conscious choice to have expectations. Some of them come from so long ago, we literally have no idea when they first began.

I remember one weekend when I had flu. Not only was it extremely inconvenient, I also hated lying there feeling my head was about to blow a gasket. But there it was—I was ill. Now there was one person who expected me at church on the Sunday who simply couldn't accept my absence. It was against all his expectations of how a pastor should behave. Where, he demanded, was Pastor Phil? On being informed I was ill in bed, he exploded, 'Pastors don't get ill!' Now don't tell me that was a grown-up response. That came from a little boy, repeating things he'd heard thirty years back about all pastors being perfect. The problem was, that unconscious expectation was now ruining the day of a forty-five-year-old man!

You, too, may have more expectations than you think. Be careful.

Out of the mouths of children

One of the things I really love about God is that he creates everyone differently. There is so much to learn about fighting the major giants in life, and yet everyone can have something to offer. Take our son Matthew. He's like no one else I've ever met. He's a happy guy, he's jolly, but he's also intriguing because even he has really been up against the system—and beaten it. He's had giant Education, and giant Institution and all sorts of amorphous grey 'powers that be' come along and threaten his creativity because he's dyslexic. But does that faze our Matthew? Not a bit of it. His faith is fantastic; and his attitude throughout has been, 'I'm not going to let that beat me, am I Dad!'

Now that's the spirit. And that should be the spirit when you're facing the system. Don't let it beat you.

Is it worth it?

So is it worth trying to defeat the giant Corporate? In
the end, *of course it's worth it!* This is a vile and heartless giant, but many people have been there before
you and won! Don't stop trying, for if there's one
thing Jesus has shown us, it's that no one—absolutely
no one—has to give in if they don't want to. Look
back on those who have gone before you. Join their
ranks—from the politicians who are succeeding in
abolishing child labour or child pornography in the
world, to the pacifists in Northern Ireland, to the fair
trade organisations like Traidcraft and Tear Fund. Let
go of worldly expectation, live in reality, and fight the
good fight!

It's only one more time

If you've been hurt once by the system, let me encourage you. Let's go again. One more time. You've
learned a lot so far, and you really can discard your
worldly expectations along with the disappointment
and frustration that follow. Your God is still your
God, and remember, your experience only adds to
your armour. Believe me, you're going to win through
for him. And it's not—repeat not—a waste of time!

You shouldn't even worry if you can't see the end
result on the horizon. Napoleon Bonaparte was once
greatly concerned that when his troops marched
down the long roads of Paris preparing for battle,
the scorching, blistering sun would beat down on
their heads and backs and have an adverse effect on
them, sapping their energies. He told his advisers that
the solution was to plant large trees on each side of

the road to give the soldiers the shade they needed to conserve their strength and be most effective in battle.

'But Sir,' said his officers, 'that would be expensive, extremely time-consuming, and it would take the best part of thirty years before the troops could possibly benefit.'

'Well, there's no time to lose, then,' said Napoleon. 'We'd better begin straight away.'

In other words, even powerful leaders can come up against the limitations of the system—in this case, the speed at which nature can produce fully grown trees! But when they keep their dreams, and refuse to accept the excuses and limitations of those around them, they will keep to their aim as easily as a baby who's determined to start walking. However many times they come across a setback, nothing is going to stop their vision in the end. And you can be the same—no matter how long it takes!

Stick to the word

Most important of all, stick close to God throughout. Joshua 1:8 urges us to 'meditate on God's word day and night'. If we do this, and follow Jesus in every way, we simply cannot fail to beat giant Negative in his corporate form. We are not mere accidents of nature. Solomon 5:16 tells us that we are 'here for such a time as this'. So hold on. Know that you, too, are born for the time and place in which you really are, and work on through it all. Prepare to go again, so that winning will become not just a possibility, but a reality in ways you never thought possible. In fact, in a blaze of God's glory!

7

The Winning Mentality

Oh that there were more Calebs around! People who 'dare to believe' are, sadly, rare. As we've just seen in the chapter about giant Corporate, life is full of people and institutions that say, 'It can't be done.' For example . . .

They said it couldn't be done but they were wrong—someone did walk on the moon.

They said it couldn't be done but they were wrong—someone did invent a machine that could fly over the Atlantic; we now live in the age of supersonic air travel.

They said it couldn't be done but they were wrong—Alexander Graham Bell did invent the telephone and today people can sit in their living rooms and hold a conversation down a wire with someone 12,000 miles away.

They said it couldn't be done but they were wrong—Roger Bannister pushed his body to the absolute limit and broke through the barrier of the four-minute mile.

They said it couldn't be done but they were wrong—a few decades ago it was unthinkable to take the healthy heart out of a dead person and transplant it in place of the decaying heart of someone still living. Thanks to Christian Barnard, it happens all over the world today.

Breakthrough people

Nassau, the Wright brothers, Alexander Graham Bell, Roger Bannister and Christian Barnard all had two things in common. First, they were all facing the so-called 'impossible, it just can't be done'. Secondly, they were all people of breakthrough. They are not alone; throughout history there have been dozens more—Esther in the Bible, Joan of Arc, Marie Curie, William Booth, Mother Teresa, Martin Luther King and Nelson Mandela, to name just a few. Such people are the visionaries, innovators and pioneers who inspire countless thousands to pursue God's purposes for the people around them. These people were willing to prove that the impossible dream could become a reality, and that impassable barriers and boundaries were only there to be broken through.

Robert Kennedy knew something of this when he said, 'Some men see things that are and say, "Why?" I dream of things that are not and say, "Why not?"'

However, such visionaries are in short supply. For every one, it seems there are also a thousand sceptics, cynics, disbelievers, scoffers and doubting Thomases, who refuse to see anything else but the negatives, the problems, the difficulties, the opposition, the cost, the workload, and the general magnitude of what they are facing—that is, the giants. Such people are basically ruled by a fear of failure which causes them to remain in their safe, secure and comfortable environments. Sadly, folk with such a mentality rarely achieve anything themselves, because the last thing they want to do is sail uncharted waters.

How different the visionary is, thriving on a new challenge and longing to go where no one has gone before. He or she is a risk-taker, a problem-solver, a possibility-thinker, a dreamer, a go-getter. When everybody says it can't be done, he or she believes it can. It calls for a different spirit altogether. Such people have a winning mentality. They refuse to let the giants succeed in their life, and they simply refuse to allow problems to swamp them. They focus, focus and focus again on the possibilities.

Sam and Jed had become fortune hunters. Five thousand dollars had been offered for each wolf captured alive. Day and night they scoured the mountains and forests looking for their valuable prey. Exhausted one night, they fell asleep dreaming of their potential fortune. Suddenly, Sam awoke to see that they were surrounded by at least fifty wolves with flaming eyes and bared teeth. He nudged his friend and said, 'Hey Jed, wake up. We're rich!'

Now that's what I call an optimist. That's the winning mentality!

A classic example

Caleb in the Old Testament is a classic example of someone who possessed that all-important winning mentality we've been talking about. He was an individual who refused to let the giants of opposition rule the day, hold him in defeat and dictate his destiny. Caleb was one very determined man.

Caleb has become one of my greatest heroes. There are many things we can learn from him concerning what it takes to win through, but I want to look at three in particular. First, he was someone who knew his calling. Secondly, he was someone who wholly followed the Lord. Thirdly, he was someone with a different spirit.

Caleb—knowing the call

The really interesting thing about Caleb is that he *was* a leader but he *wasn't* a number one. He always played second fiddle and was someone else's assistant, functioning best in ministry in a supporting role. He was an ideal number two. As far as we know, he was happy and fulfilled and a most productive leader in this capacity. And the lovely thing is, he never even tried to take on the number one position. He knew what God had called him to do and he was content in doing it.

I've always thought Caleb had a brilliant attitude about service in the kingdom of God. There is something delightfully refreshing about it. You see, many people in church life have a calling in their lives to leadership, but they miss it by assuming it means leading from a number one position. But God may well be calling them to be like Caleb, and to be a leader serving as a number two. Indeed, I have met many a minister who is struggling and totally frustrated because they are trying to function as 'the visionary—the leader' whereas in reality God has actually called them to be a part of a team and to minister in a supportive role. Let me make this point quite clearly: there is nothing second rate or inferior about serving God as a number two, or even three or four or twenty-four for that matter.

Leadership—a touchy subject

I appreciate that leadership can be a very delicate and touchy area, especially when there are those in our fellowships who would take advantage by telling the minister or leader that he or she is 'only' a number two and forcing them out so that they can take over the leadership themselves. How people believe God can bless such a move is totally beyond me. Spiritual coups never work. However, the fact still remains that the kingdom of God would advance far better if we all knew exactly what God had called us to, and if we were confident in the fulfilment of that calling.

Knowing where God has placed you and the responsibility to which he has called you is a crucial factor in whether you will win through and achieve for God. At the end of the day it is only the clear call of God that will keep you faithful and pressing on towards your goal when the going gets tough. It is immaterial whether you are in a position that is seen or not. It is where God wants you and what he wants you to be engaged in that is the all-important issue, for it is here that you will be most content, fulfilled and productive for God.

Caleb's specific role

Caleb knew that the specific role God had called him to was to support and complement Joshua's overall leadership. He saw his ministry as an extension of Joshua's ministry. As Elisha was to Elijah, so Caleb was to Joshua and he was more than happy to serve in that position to the best of his God-given ability. Some people are certainly called to serve as a second in command, just as Caleb was. If you are one such person, don't stoop to be a king (or for that matter a number one), for you have a high calling indeed.

By the way, don't let the giant of Self-pity con you into thinking that by ministering as a number two you will miss out on all the action. That is another of Satan's downright lies. In God, Caleb achieved some amazing victories and earned himself the reputation of being a mighty giant-killer. God caused Caleb to triumph against almost insurmountable odds and caused him to be significant in his own right, serving the purposes of God in his own generation.

However, there is a price to pay. There has to be sacrifice—the giving of life over to God. Many people through the years have made the mistake of committing themselves to the *work* of God and allowing this to become a poor substitute for a real relationship with God himself. Caleb knew there could be no substitute or compromise where this issue was concerned, and he committed himself wholly to following the Lord. Being determined to win through and reach your goal is one thing; being determined to know God is something else altogether. The latter is far more important!

Caleb—wholly following the Lord

Caleb was a 110 per cent person, if ever there was one. The outstanding qualities that continually shine through when you study this man's character are his faithfulness, commitment and singlemindedness towards knowing God. He was faithful to God from the start and he continued to be so throughout his entire life, still unwavering even in old age. It is recorded in the Bible on at least six occasions that

Caleb 'wholly followed the Lord' and because of this he was able to possess the Promised Land (Num 14:24; 32:11–12; Deut 1:36; Josh 14:8–9; 14:14). You realise what a tremendous accolade this is when you consider that it was God himself who said this. Wholeheartedness is obviously a quality that means a lot to God.

But just what does it mean in practice to 'wholly follow the Lord'? The word 'wholly' means fully, completely, utterly, thoroughly, absolutely, comprehensively, totally, unreservedly, exclusively, steadfastly and uncompromisingly. All these words describe exactly how Caleb followed the Lord. He was emphatically wholehearted. This meant he gave his time, talents, finances, relationships, work, emotions, will, family, leisure, devotional life—in fact, every area of his life whether it was public or private—over to God.

A quick trip to the New Testament

Allow me to take you for a few moments to the New Testament. You will remember how on one occasion in Matthew's Gospel a lawyer asked Jesus a question, thinking he might catch him out: 'What is the greatest commandment?' Jesus replied, 'You shall love the Lord your God with all your heart, with all your soul and with all your mind.' This answer is a direct quote from the Old Testament, Deuteronomy 6:5, which instructs us to love and serve God with every fibre of our being. For Caleb this was a living reality. He regarded his relationship with God as being of paramount importance. In him he quite literally 'lived, moved and had his being'.

Now the opposite of 'wholly' is partly, moderately,

haphazardly, occasionally, halfheartedly and compromisingly. These words were simply not in Caleb's vocabulary at all and they were definitely not a part of his make-up. No way was he prepared to compromise his walk with God. Even when all of Israel, apart from his friend Joshua, turned their back on God in unbelief, he remained 'steadfast and immovable, always abounding in the work of the Lord'.

Psalm 78 tells us that the children of Israel often rebelled against God in the wilderness. They were a generation whose spirit was not faithful to God; they were not steadfast towards him; and they were not faithful in keeping his covenant. Instead, they actually pained and grieved the Holy One of Israel. It was in the midst of this hostile environment lasting over forty years that Caleb made his stand virtually alone. No one is saying it is easy to stand alone, but sometimes it is absolutely necessary. To conduct a symphony you must turn your back on the crowd.

When you think about it, there must have been many times when Caleb came under a lot of pressure from his peers. 'Hey, Caleb, don't rock the boat. Just go with the flow, man. Life's too short. Don't take it so seriously. Enjoy yourself. After all, we can't all be wrong!' To Caleb's credit he was having none of it.

To wholly follow the Lord takes huge quantities of determination, tenacity and personal discipline. Now lots of people can do it when everything is going according to plan and when things are on the up; when they're standing on praise mountain, full of faith and believing in God for absolutely anything. But how different it can be when God seems a million miles away, when nothing seems to be happening, when the chips are down and you've suffered a setback or two and discouragement has set in. To be wholehearted means to be faithful even in these times and Caleb knew this.

Have a spiritual check-up

Second Chronicles 6:14 says, 'O Lord God of Israel, there is no God in heaven or on earth like You, who keep Your covenant and mercy with Your servants who walk before You with all their hearts.'

Now be careful to catch the last phrase there. It says that God shows mercy, blessing and favour to those who walk before him 'with all their hearts'. It could just as easily say 'Those who walk before him wholeheartedly.' If we want to receive God's grace then we would all do well to take an honest and unbiased appraisal of our relationship with him. A sort of 'personal spiritual check-up', giving God the opportunity to speak into our lives.

Ask yourself, 'Am I walking before God with all my heart? Is there any area of my life where there is compromise? Am I withholding any area of my life from God? Is there any area I want to control and keep for myself?' Be open to the Holy Spirit. Ask him to show you if there are any areas in your life that need immediate attention. Jesus promised us in John 14:15–17 and John 16:12 that the Holy Spirit would be committed to counselling, teaching, helping and guiding us in all truth.

The key to getting answers to prayer

Let me tell you why it is important to take this personal spiritual check-up. When you aren't living for God wholeheartedly, it affects your personal faith level. If you look at 1 John 3:20–22 you will read,

'For if our heart condemns us, God is greater than our heart, and knows all things. Beloved, if our heart does not condemn us, we have confidence toward God. And whatever we ask we receive from Him, because we keep His commandments and do those things that are pleasing in His sight.'

You see, it is not what God knows about you that keeps your prayers from being answered. It is not what your husband or your wife knows about you or anybody else for that matter. It is not what the devil knows about you. It is what you know about yourself! When you know you're not living for God and doing what you know you should do, you don't have any confidence towards him and approaching him becomes difficult to say the least. You can almost become embarrassed to face him.

But if you are honouring him and following him wholeheartedly, both in the good times and the bad; if your heart does not condemn you, then a great confidence rises within you, a confidence that no devil or giant can shake. It is a confidence that nobody can talk you out of and no pressure, no matter how great, can force you into letting go. It is a confidence that enables you to ask and believe God for absolutely anything; a confidence that creates an expectancy and spurs you on to attempt and win great things for God.

The bottom line is simply this: when God finds someone who is available and loyal to him, he always proves himself available and loyal to them. This is made abundantly clear in 1 Samuel 2:30, where it says, '. . . those who honor me I will honor.' Now you can't get any plainer than that, can you?

Another fascinating verse in this respect is

2 Chronicles 16:9. It says, 'For the eyes of the Lord run to and fro throughout the whole earth, to show Himself strong on behalf of those whose heart is loyal to Him.' The Authorised version uses the word 'perfect', but it doesn't refer, as you might think, to someone who has got it all together and who doesn't make mistakes. It actually means one who is available, loyal, faithful and wholehearted. God is constantly searching for opportunities to show himself strong on our behalf! However, he is looking for those who will apply themselves to being wholehearted towards himself, just like Caleb.

Caleb—a person with a new spirit

Caleb had another tremendous quality. He had no problem at all in believing in God for great things. Woe betide anyone who told him, 'It can't be done!' He just refused point blank to accept it. He constantly refused to let anyone set the boundaries of his faith, preferring to believe that with God all things were possible. Oh that there were more Calebs around— people who 'dare to believe'! Now you know why I began this chapter with those very words. I believe the church today needs men and women more than ever who have the Caleb spirit, who know God, know their calling and, as I have said before, firmly lay hold of that for which God has laid hold of them.

In Numbers 14:24, Caleb is actually described by God as being a man with a 'different spirit'—a spirit that said it could be done when everyone else said it couldn't; a spirit that said it was possible when everyone was shouting 'Impossible'; a spirit that said 'Let's go for it,' when everyone else was crying 'Hold fire'; a spirit that said 'God will provide,' when everyone was shouting 'Recession'. Caleb's thinking certainly cut against the grain of popular opinion, and his example is quite inspiring.

Behind enemy lines

Let's pick up Caleb's story in Numbers 13, where we find the Israelites wandering in the wilderness, trapped and hemmed in by their disobedience and unbelief. However, they were now on the verge of realising their dream of many years—possessing the Promised Land.

Moses chose twelve men to go on a fact-finding mission and spy out the land. Now these weren't just any men; they were leaders, twelve of the very best. They were supposed to be men of considerable talent, skill and ability. Moses had a briefing session with his special 'crack team' and informed them exactly what facts and information he required, and off they went on their forty-day reconnaissance mission behind enemy lines.

On their return they reported back to Moses and the other Israelites. All twelve unanimously agreed that the land was rich and plentiful, and that indeed it was a land flowing with milk and honey. They could see all the advantages and could give plenty of good reasons why they should enter the land. They even brought samples of Canaan's lip-smacking, thirst-quenching, finger-licking fruit back with them, a sort of taster of good things to come. Without dispute it was a truly magnificent country.

The amazing thing is, ten of the spies concluded their reports with a negative emphasis. All they seemed interested in was why they wouldn't be able to go up and possess the land. They majored on all the problems and obstacles in the way. All that filled their minds now were the fortified cities with great walls, and the giants who stood on the walls as territorial guards—giants and walls they'd never seen the like of before that seemed bigger than big and stronger than strong. These giants had muscles in places where the Israelites didn't even have places! The spies explained how the giants looked every bit undefeated champions and intimidatingly terrifying. In their own eyes, they even admitted that they felt like mere grasshoppers in comparison. They felt there was no way they could win, and they would be foolish even to try. Like a contagious disease, fear swept the camp. The Israelites, like so many people before and since, talked and worried themselves into defeat before they'd even begun.

Caleb and Joshua's position

As for the other two spies, Caleb and Joshua, they just couldn't believe what they were hearing. They too had seen exactly what the others had seen. They too had witnessed with their own eyes the strength of the giants and the size of the walls. They too had seen Canaan's vast array of weaponry. They too had seen all the hurdles that lay before them, just as their timid companions had.

But in the midst of all this Caleb and Joshua could see something else which to them was far more significant. They could see God in it all which meant they focused on and were excited by nothing but the possibilities. They were men full of faith who dared to believe that God would overcome every difficulty and barrier. Giants and walled cities didn't intimidate Caleb. He exercised the type of faith that expects God to keep his promises and the type of faith that showed he was in active relationship with God.

The new spirit arises

Enter Caleb! He simply couldn't stay quiet any longer. He was just bursting, determined to speak some faith into the situation: 'We should by all means go up and take possession for we shall surely overcome.' Caleb knew that this was not a time for shrinking back; this was the time for pressing on and going for all that God had for them. Now that's a person with a new spirit talking.

Why was Caleb right?

Caleb was more than aware that the type of giants they were talking about here were the descendants of Anak and Amalek. Many would have been between seven and nine feet tall by all accounts. He was also aware that the imposing walls surrounding the cities in question were thirty or more feet high. When it came to Canaan's arsenal he knew it was far more advanced and effective than Israel's.

With all this in mind Caleb no doubt felt the Israelites' fear was understandable, but he still didn't see it as justifiable. After all, hadn't the all-powerful, most high God, the God who had parted the Red Sea and delivered them from the Egyptians' hand, promised to be with them and lead them into victory once again? Caleb knew, as we all do really, that God never has a problem backing up his word. The only problem he ever has is finding people who will believe it and walk with it.

Caleb was no dummy, either. He knew that by worldly standards Israel's army was no great shakes. In terms of military power they were well down the list. But surely the decisive factor here was that God was on their side? Caleb had learned that it was not whether you are the biggest, the strongest, the richest or the best that counts, but whether or not God is with you. It is the same today where you and I are concerned. It doesn't matter what opposition or circumstances we come up against, if we are truly working for and in relationship with God, he is with us and we need fear nothing. Caleb was not so much confident in Israel's ability to wage war and conquer the land. His confidence and boldness rested on his position in God. Whereas the Israelites focused on their limited human strength, Caleb had got his eyes firmly fixed on God's infinite resources and power. That's why he was right.

Eighty-five and still going strong

Caleb was eighty-five years of age when he finally inherited his portion of the Promised Land, forty-five years after God had originally given him the promise. By this time, all Caleb's generation had died except Joshua and himself. They had survived the 'wilderness wanderings' and deaths on the battlefields of Canaan.

But the passage of time had not dimmed their faith and spiritual vision one bit. Caleb continued to 'wholly follow' the Lord and as a result was as strong in his latter years as he was when he was forty. He was still able and willing to face the giants at eighty-five, when we find him pleading with God,

'Give me this mountain' (Hebron—his portion of the inheritance).

Even as an octogenarian Caleb had faith to believe in God for the 'high' strategic places. He went on to fight the giants and defeat them. Now I don't know how he did it—maybe he hit them with his zimmer frame—but one thing's for sure: he kept believing in God even in the toughest times and came out on top. There's someone with a right attitude. There's someone with a different spirit. There's a winner.

Now is the time

If ever there was a generation that needed to press on to the things of God and possess the land, it's ours. If ever there was a time we needed men and women with the Caleb spirit, it's now. This is not the time for shrinking back and being passive. It is the time for courageously going forward with faith in God to pull down strongholds, defy the giants and press on and take the land.

- Now is the time to build big churches.
- Now is the time to birth new churches.
- Now is the time to be significant in your place of work.
- Now is the time to develop great social projects that reach into the community.
- Now is the time to let the people of your area know that God's people are in town and they're not going to go away.
- Now is the time to break the mould.
- Now is the time to do something wonderful for God.
- Now is the time to go for it.

So:

1. Make a quality decision to be like Caleb of old: know your calling and be careful to walk in it.
2. Know God, completely give yourself over to him and wholly follow his word.
3. In the midst of a negative world, be determined to be a person with a different spirit and defeat the giants and possess your mountain.

Add these three ingredients together and you've got the winning mentality.

Zig Ziglar, that excellent motivational and inspirational author and speaker, said in his book *Over the Top*, 'Every man, woman, young person and child is designed for accomplishment, engineered for success and endowed with the seeds of greatness.' And the wonderful thing is—we're all included. So go for it!

8

You Too Can Win

The eight men got down as the person with the pistol
stood firm. In that split second, which seemed to last
an hour, a deadly hush descended, and at the very
same moment the events of the last few months
flashed through their minds.

All that agony, pain, loneliness and waiting—not to
mention the sheer guts and determination that caused
them to hang in there in the hope that one day they
would win through. This was the only thing that had
kept them going. Often they felt they'd come to the
end, having nothing more to give, but always there
was something inside urging and pushing them to
press on and not give in. They'd all proved time
and time again that they possessed deep hidden
resources that could be drawn upon in the most tax-
ing of circumstances; that all-important little bit extra
that wills a person through.

Hearts pounded and muscles tightened. One false
move could spell sure disaster. Suddenly, one of the
eight tried to break away. The person with the pistol
fired a shot and he froze in his tracks and was quickly
ushered back into line. He was told if it happened
again he was finished. The tension, the pressure, was
palpable. Then, it happened. The man with the pistol

135

fired another shot . . . and the eight athletes bolted out of their starting blocks with nothing but gold and victory in sight. Just one thing was clear: there's no glory to be had in losing, only in winning!

Those like Caleb who are determined to win in life give nothing less than 110 per cent. Their attitude is one of total commitment, one of wholeheartedness. They know there can be no real satisfaction in not doing their absolute best. They live to win. Just ask any athlete who means business.

Winners never settle for the status quo; they are never happy with a mediocre life. They are always willing to work that little bit harder, give that little bit extra, go that little bit further, dig that little bit deeper, pushing themselves beyond their previous limits to achieve their dreams and aspirations. They are also willing to pay the price—the time, effort and utter single-mindedness may cost them dear—but the rewards are fantastic! Consequently, when true winners are confronted by the giants of opposition, they have a quite extraordinary ability to press on with the kind of creative force that pushes every obstacle out of the way. They believe that nothing is too difficult for God and they believe that all things are possible—even the 'impossible'.

So what does it take?

What does it take to be a winner? Everyone wants to know the answer to that question. Everyone wants to win. But when it comes right down to where the rubber meets the road, not everyone is willing to pay the price.

Let's just think about this for a minute. The word

'price', associated with athletes, conjures up great macho images of tough training sessions, masses of sweat, loads of rippling muscles, beating the clock, that kind of thing. But in Christian terms, it's less of a Hollywood picture. Everyone talks about the second mile, but very few talk about the first mile. If you like, 'price' in Christian terms is about doing that grim first mile to the very best of your ability, as well as the much applauded second mile. It's the 10.30 pm session to do the ironing although you're dog-tired; it's the 'nth' hour more with the vagrant who's sitting there weeping over the ashes of his life; it's the keeping of one's temper with a parent who has Alzheimer's and who asks yet again what's for supper; it's the prayer to the Lord when it's the last thing you feel like doing.

In 1 Corinthians Paul challenges us to run in such a way as to win. He goes on to say that winning doesn't just happen. To be a winner a person must exude certain qualities and characteristics: determination, dedication, diligence, discipline, self-denial, persistence and application, not just physically and mentally but spiritually as well. Paul uses the illustration of the athlete and goes on to explain how they train and live to win. Athletes never become winners by merely observing from the grandstand, and neither do they just jog a couple of laps around the block each morning when the weather is fine. Winners give their all. Sometimes they train for years to break through. They decide to go for gold—no matter what the cost—and they refuse to let anyone or anything stand in the way. But the illustration of the athlete should not delude us. Sometimes the Christian way is completely unglorious in worldly terms—a way that Paul

himself knew only too well. Sometimes it's just ago-
nisingly hard.

What it all adds up to is this. Paul was saying that if
you want to take hold of your God-given dreams and
make them a reality, then you are going to have to be
just as determined as that winning athlete—more so,
in fact, because you are running to receive nothing
less than the prize of your high calling in Christ Jesus.
That's exactly the kind of determination and effort it
takes to win through. This is how the apostle Paul put
it at the end of 1 Corinthians 9 if you look in Eugene
Peterson's *The Message* (the New Testament in con-
temporary English):

> You've all been to the stadium and seen the athletes race.
> Everyone runs; one wins. Run to win. All good athletes
> train hard. They do it for a gold medal that tarnishes and
> fades. You're after one that's gold eternally. I don't know
> about you, but I'm running hard for the finish line. I'm
> giving it everything I've got. No sloppy living for me! I'm
> staying alert and in top condition. I'm not going to get
> caught napping, telling everyone else about it and then
> missing out myself.

Jesus spoke about this type of determination in Matthew 11:12 when he said, '. . . the kingdom of heaven
suffers violence, and the violent take it by force'. Here
Jesus was talking about laying hold of the kingdom of
God on earth today, taking hold of the blessings of
God and your promised inheritance by faith. It's
something that's never easy. The majority of people
just don't see faith as a violent force, they see it as
something passive and personal. But if you want to
achieve, win through and take hold of those promises

of God, then Jesus says that your faith will have to become violent. It has to be done by force.

Now of course Jesus doesn't mean this in a bodily aggressive way but rather by being spiritually determined. Real faith is active. It is spiritually aggressive. It takes the word of God and uses it as a weapon to bring down every spiritual giant and stronghold of doubt and unbelief. It breaks through every obstacle in its way!

Too many Christians and churches waste their time just hanging around and drifting through life with a passive faith, believing God will do everything for them. They are literally spectators in the arena of life, expecting God to do all the running. It simply doesn't work this way. If we're going to win over the giants then we've got to run against them. And we've got to be determined to run well. Indeed, what a person believes and his or her determination to act on it is the difference between the impossible and the possible, between winning or losing.

Did you ever see *Chariots of Fire*, the award winning film about the two runners, Harold Abrahams and Eric Liddell, and their build-up to the 1924 Olympic Games? If you did you will recall that both men were determined to win. In one of the pre-Olympic preparation races, Abrahams and Liddell find themselves yet again racing against each other. On this occasion Liddell won. Abrahams was so deflated and discouraged by the defeat that he was ready to throw in the towel. As his girlfriend tried to console and encourage him, in his disappointment and frustration he shouted, 'I run to win. If I don't win, I don't run.'

'And if you don't run, you won't win,' she replied.

He did run again and he did win. In fact, both men came back with gold medals. You see, winners always decide to run, and they always run to win.

What's the plan?

Next, let us consider another crucial characteristic that winners have. Before we even think about training to win, we need to think about what we're trying to win in the first place. It is vitally important that we know this. If you want to be one of God's winners, make sure your plans are in tandem with God's plans for your life. Unless you've got this particular truth in place, all your efforts will be nothing but frustratingly futile.

In Andrew Lloyd Webber's hit musical, *Joseph and His Amazing Technicolored Dreamcoat*, one of the lines Joseph sings in the lead song says, 'Any dream will do.' Although I love the musical and it's wonderfully inspiring, this one line by Tim Rice has missed the target by a million miles. 'Any dream' won't do! For your dream and your heart's desire to become a reality, it's got to be the right dream—God's dream for you.

Hear me right now: there is nothing wrong with dreaming. In fact, I wish people would dream more. Not only that; as it doesn't cost anything to dream big or small, I believe we might as well dream big. Indeed, we have an omnipotent, almighty God through whom all things are possible. But nevertheless, if we are going to achieve anything for God then the dreams we pursue must fall right in line with God's plan and purpose for our lives. The book of Proverbs tells us, 'Many are the plans in a person's heart, but it is the counsel of the Lord that will prevail.' Jeremiah 29:11 also tells us that God has a plan for every one of us. But the big question is: How can we know and know for sure what God's will is? Just what is his plan for our lives?

The passage itself goes on to answer: 'You must seek the Lord.' It tells us that we will find him when 'we search for him with all our hearts'. Doesn't this sound vaguely reminiscent of what Jesus said in Matthew 7:7: 'Ask and it will be given to you, seek and you will find, knock and it will be opened to you'?

I can almost hear someone objecting, 'But surely it doesn't matter what I'm doing for God, as long as I am doing something. After all, "all things work together for good to those that love the Lord", don't they?'

This verse in Romans 8:28 is used and bantered around a lot, but it is so often only half-quoted. People either ignorantly or conveniently omit the last part of the verse. What it says in full is, 'And we know that all things work together for good to those who love the Lord, *who are called according to his purpose.*' In other words, all things will come together, working together for good to profit the kingdom of God, when we are walking in and pursuing his divine purpose and plan. As Psalm 127:1 says, 'Unless the Lord builds the house, they labor in vain who build it.' To put it bluntly, 'If he ain't in it, forget it;' you are simply barking up the wrong tree.

Let me give you an example. I know a happily married Christian couple, whom we'll call Mike and Judy, who were convinced that they would be good parents. They were certain God wanted them to have children and bring them up in a loving and creative home. There was a problem of infertility, so they were trying new medical methods of conception at their local hospital. Over the next four years, there were four pregnancies, but they all failed. Naturally, the miscarriages caused great sadness and hurt, but for Mike and Judy there was also another overriding feeling: they were puzzled. They felt so strongly that they could and should be parents—it was part of their Christian mission.

So they became even more determined to pray and wait on God. And one memorable day, God spoke to them. Judy puts it this way: 'It was during that prayer—you know, the one that goes, "Let me be full, let me be empty, let me have all things, let me have nothing; I freely and wholeheartedly yield all things to your pleasure and disposal . . . ." And suddenly God took charge. It was as if he very gently and quietly put a hand over my mouth. He hushed all my questions; he even stopped me thinking. It was like being in a vacuum, but a good one. And then he just said, very softly: "You are still right; you are still to be parents. But it has to be my way, not yours. Let go of all these pursuits, and wait on me."

'It's funny, we were planning another try that summer, and we were sure it would be fine this time. But God was quite clear. We were to stop following our own courses of treatment, and we were to wait on him. So we did. We just stopped trying to "play God". Instead, we just put our trust in him.

'Just three weeks later, someone we hardly knew sent us a cutting quite out of the blue from the local paper. It was about the desperate need for adoptive parents in our own particular district, for certain specific children. And we just knew this was it. That was ten years ago. We now have four adopted children and one foster child, and sometimes it's so hard I wonder whether we were dotty to think we'd be the slightest bit good at it in the first place. But it still feels right. It is God's purpose for us.'

Judy and Mike are real winners (and by the way, their kids are just great!) because they battled on against every obstacle to fulfil what they believed was right for them. But the biggest win of all was finding out what God's purpose for them was, so they could prepare and train for the race they had to run.

If you're not sure where you're heading and what God wants for your life, this would be my best advice to you. Take the next exit off the road you're on, park up for a while and earnestly seek God's face so that you might get on the right road, and know for sure where you are heading in God and how to get there. Spend time in prayer and fasting and get into his word and I guarantee he'll direct you. 'Your word is a lamp to my feet and a light for my path' (Ps 119:105). Whatever it takes, be willing to pay the price—the time and the effort—of finding out God's unique plan for you. It's your responsibility to tap into it and not just once, but continually, at every stage in your life.

Winners have the right attitude

Once you have God's purpose in place, you can concentrate on the next thing: being a winner also depends on having the right attitude. First, you will need the right attitude towards the way God feels about you. God is absolutely committed to you, and to his purposes for your life and your success. He knows you can achieve great things for him. He believes in you and has total confidence in you because he believes you're an absolute winner.

Secondly, it's just as important to have the right attitude about yourself. Now it's time I introduced you to another giant, the 'Not Me' giant. This particular giant excels in its deceitful and sneaky occupation of peddling all sorts of defeatist, pessimistic, inferior and unbalanced attitudes. Its sole mission in life is subtly to infiltrate a person's heart and mind, getting them to say, 'Not me. God is never on my side. In fact I doubt if he even knows I exist. He certainly isn't interested in me and he never talks to me. Not little me.'

'Not Me' tactics

Unfortunately there are hosts of people, including many, many Christians, who have allowed themselves to fall victim to this wicked, sly giant. Not Me succeeds time and time again in persuading people that they are not really important to God and God doesn't much care whether they succeed or fail, win or lose. Sometimes such people even believe they will never succeed or win because God is intent on punishing them for some past sin. They have come to believe that their lot in life is to be nothing but the victim and not a victor.

If you think I'm joking, I'm not; I'm deadly serious. The Not Me giant can hold people very tightly in its torturous grip. It purveys all types of negative and destructive rubbish specifically designed to destroy a person's self-esteem and eradicate the concept of what he or she could achieve or is capable of. It downplays the positives and highlights the negatives, and it insists on trying to limit you, telling you that you could never in a million years rise above the status quo. Its whole *raison d'être* is to stop you from winning through and successfully achieving, and to thwart the purposes of God.

So watch out carefully for this giant and its devious ways. It is subtle. It will even try to convince you that winning isn't important anyway. It even persuades people to believe that it is totally unbiblical to win because it smacks of competitiveness and selfish ambition. This couldn't be further from the truth. God made each of us to succeed with him. He created each one of us in his image to win and win big—to win spiritually, not only in religious life but also in relationships, finances, career and every other area. In fact, I'd even dare to go a step further: if you're not intent on winning, then you are not really fulfilling God's whole purpose for your life.

The devil is an expert at getting people to believe that God is not really on their side and therefore they are doomed to fail. But if we are to be winners and victorious, then we must take heed of the word of God where it boldly declares in Psalm 118:6, 'The Lord is with me. He is on my side.' God is for us and is absolutely committed to our success, and his one desire is to lead us into victory. When you realise that God is really for you, and when you let this one truth sink deep inside of you, then you will soon realise that the sky is the limit. The world is your oyster and all things can become possible in God.

Now listen again to what Jeremiah 29:11 says concerning you and your future. 'I know the plans I have for you, declares the Lord, plans for welfare and not for calamity, to give you a future and a hope' (NASB). That certainly sounds like a God who is on our side. As Mike and Judy found out for themselves, God's plan for us is a plan for no less than our true success. A plan for winning over every giant that comes our way. So don't let the Not Me giant get to you. Know this one thing and know it well: God is on your side and he does want you to win.

Eureka!

Once you have the right attitude about God, and the way he feels about you—and, of course, the right attitude about yourself—it suddenly all comes together. You'll suddenly cry 'Eureka!' and start seeing yourself as God sees you—an absolute winner. Remind yourself of God's word where it says, 'No weapon formed against you can prosper and no word said against you can stand.' Be encouraged. If God really is for you, then nothing and no one can successfully come against you. You have God's word on it!

Of course, bad times will still occur—when you falter, when you have to stop and do something over again, when you doubt your ability to win (and defeat the giants of life). But if you determine in your heart to keep your attitudes right, you will win in the end! The apostle Paul knew this when he boldly declared, 'I can do all things through Christ who strengthens me.' Apply your heart; lay hold of that for which Christ has laid hold of you; and win!

Academics at Harvard University in the USA once studied in depth the reasons why people succeed and win through in life. The results were absolutely fascinating. They revealed that no less than 85 per cent of the reasons for success, accomplishments, achievements, promotions, and so on, were that people had the right attitudes. Only 15 per cent of the reasons were attributed to technical expertise and skill. It seems pretty conclusive from these results that attitude is far more important than aptitude. Certain psychologists believe that the most important discovery of our time is that we can alter our lives by altering our attitude. I think they've got a point! Having an attitude problem is only for losers. You see, your attitude will ultimately determine your altitude.

Winners always shoot for excellence

Another characteristic of an overcomer and a giant-killer is that the hallmark of excellence always marks everything he or she does. Now this is a vital ingredient in the recipe for success, especially as we seem to be living more and more in an 'anything will do' era, when people think 'What is the least I can possibly get away with?' Some folk just don't want to see that the difference between ordinary and extraordinary is that little 'extra'. The plain truth is that there is no excuse for poor quality, and there is no substitute for the pursuit of excellence. In the long run, excellence always pays off.

But what exactly is excellence? Can it be measured? Surely one person's excellence is another person's mediocrity? The best definition I have ever come across is this:

Excellence is going far beyond the call of duty. It is doing more than others expect; this is what excellence is all about. It comes from striving for and maintaining the highest standards, looking after the smallest detail and always going the extra mile. Excellence means doing your very best in everything—in every way.

You will find that excellence never just 'happens'. It's never an accident. It is always a result of high intention, positive effort and clear direction, along with plenty of skilful execution. It's about really giving your best, attending to the little things and sweating over the small stuff. It's about doing things right, not 'nearly right'. You don't do half a job, you finish the job. Remember David in the Old Testament? He not only knocked Goliath off his feet, he cut off his ugly head, making doubly sure this giant would never rise again. He finished the job thoroughly. That's what excellence is.

Moreover, excellence always represents wisdom— the best and wisest choice of many options. In my opinion, one of the unwritten laws of life says that excellence and good things happen when they are planned. Inferiority and bad activities don't need planning, they happen by default! People of excellence, however, fully understand that today's preparation determines tomorrow's achievements and successes.

Ian Botham, the internationally famous all-round cricketer, was once asked in an interview how he prepared for defeat and failure. His answer was simple and to the point. 'I don't,' he said. 'I only ever train to win.' Now that's what it's all about.

Excellence is all about doing your best for God and attaining your maximum potential in God. But it also has something to do with reaching beyond and surpassing your normal grasp. Winners and giant-killers are often people who choose to commit their ideas and energies to causes that are much bigger than themselves. So let me throw down the gauntlet. Let me challenge you to out-perform yourself. You should always have goals that stretch you. Goals that are big enough to get the very best out of you.

Excellence in the church?

Why is excellence in such short supply and such a rare commodity in the church? Why do we so often insist, time and time again, in giving our second best when it comes to our time, money, possessions, work and service where the kingdom of God is concerned? Over the years I have noticed in particular how many Christians seem to delight in becoming extremely generous when it comes to giving God their cast-offs. There isn't a minister in the country, or for that matter in the world, who hasn't had an offer of someone's throw-aways.

'Pastor, I was going to throw away this old fridge. You see we've had it for fifteen years or more. We bought it nearly new and it really is time we had a new one. But then I thought the church could do with one. So you can have it. I knew you'd be pleased. All it needs is a new thermostat and, oh yes, it leaks a little. But it will do for the church. Mind you, you'll have to call and collect it. It's in the garbage, I mean the garage.'

What is it that gets us to believe that such a thing is an acceptable offering to the Lord? How can we say 'It's good enough—it's only for the church!' or, 'It will do for now. I haven't got time to do it properly'? If I haven't got time to do it properly now, how on earth will I ever find time to do it over again?

It's about time we made sure our 'good enough' is good enough for the King of Glory. He deserves nothing but our best. If Jesus were truly sitting in your living-room, would you hand him the cracked plate with the stale crisps? I bet you wouldn't. But Jesus *is* in your sitting-room. He's in mine, he's on the pavement outside my house, he's inside my church, outside my church, he's everywhere in my life. And he's everywhere in yours. We should aim for the highest of standards, not the easy conscience-salvers.

So what are we to do? The writer Orison S. Marden says, 'It's a matter of just making your mind up at the very outset that all your work is going to stand for quality. See to it that you stamp a superior quality on everything that goes out of your hands, that whatever you do shall bear the hallmark of excellence.'

In one of his great rallying speeches Martin Luther King, Jr, said, 'If a man is called to be a street-sweeper, he should sweep streets as Michelangelo painted or Beethoven composed music. He should sweep streets so well that all the hosts of heaven and earth will pause to say, "Here lived a great street-sweeper who did his job well."'

Don't you think we all need to live beyond the level of mediocrity? Don't you think it's time to raise the standard? Excellence must always be our hallmark and we should settle for nothing less. Someone once said, 'Every job is a self-portrait of the person who did it, so make sure you autograph your work with quality.' Henry Beecher wrote, 'It's up to you to hold yourself responsible for higher standards than any-body else expects of you.'

Why not make a quality decision for life right now? Make a commitment to be the best and do the best you possibly can in God and continue to develop what you have. It's funny how it works, but when you give of your best God somehow makes it the best. Excellence, like winning, is a day-by-day, minute-by-minute, second-by-second, person-by-person challenge. Today the challenge is yours. Shoot for excellence! This is the type of stuff winners and giant-killers are made of.

9

Don't Quit

Great! You've decided the winning mentality is for you and that with God's help you too can do it. I honour you for making this decisive step in your walk with God. The next bit, however, is the follow-through, and let me warn you—the going will not always be easy. You see, the devil will see how serious you are and he is going to do his level best to turn up the heat!

Never a truer saying was uttered than this: 'Quitters never win, and winners never quit.' These basic truths affect the entire human race, including you, whoever you are and whatever you believe. So the purpose of this chapter is to develop some ideas about how not to quit when those giants seem to have the upper hand.

To begin with, it's worth recognising that some people do give up all too easily. It is not an uncommon thing to want to do; believe me, everyone feels like quitting at some point. It's never the answer, but there's no doubt that occasionally it can look quite an attractive option. Take Rosie, for example, a smart single lady in her late thirties, who came to see me at the office one day.

'Hello, Rosie,' I said. 'How are you?'

'Well actually, Pastor, I have a prayer request,' she answered. 'I am out of work you see and I definitely need to find a job. Could you please get the church to pray that the right door will open.'

I willingly agreed and later the church set about praying. A few weeks later, she burst into my office again, this time beaming with a smile from ear to ear.

'Pastor, guess what! I've just been for an interview as a secretary with a local firm and I've got the job and I start on Monday. I'm sure it's of God.'

'Praise God,' I said, and so we rejoiced together and when the church heard about it they were obviously thrilled with yet another affirmative answer to their prayers.

But three weeks later, Helen and I were shopping in the town when we just happened to meet up with Rosie.

'Hey, how's the new job going?' I asked.

'Well to be honest with you, Pastor, I've just given in my notice.'

'You've *what*?' I said. 'Why?'

'Pastor, you wouldn't believe it. They were such a godless bunch. They did nothing but swear, gossip, smoke and tell dirty jokes. There was no way I was going to put up with that. It's certainly no environment for a Spirit-filled Christian to be in. So I had no alternative. I resigned. Honestly, Pastor, I've never been in such a God-forsaken hole. It was as if the devil himself worked there.'

'Now let me get this right, Rosie. You get the whole church praying for you that God will find you a job. He provides you with a job and you believe it really is of him, and three weeks later you pack it in because the people in the office do what some non-Christians do anyway.'

'Well, yes, that's about the measure of it. But what else could I do? There is no way God would want me in the middle of all that. I just had to make my stand.'

'Rosie,' I said, not a little challenged, 'for goodness' sake, why do you think God put you there in the first place? He wanted you to be salt and light. He put you there so that he could bring a change through you and so that you could lead these people to Christ.'

But sadly Rosie couldn't hack it, and she wasn't going back. She just wouldn't accept that God had put her there to bring his kingdom into that place. She reckoned she knew best and that dropping out was her only option. She refused to trust God and hang in there, shining her light in the darkest places and bringing life, believing that he would see her through. So it never happened. Instead, she bowed down to the clever tactics of a giant called Quit.

However, even if Rosie didn't realise this for herself, her story still has some important lessons for the rest of us.

First, we should never get all uppity about the fact that some non-Christians do non-Christian things. Some people do swear, some do enjoy a dirty joke, many do gossip and have affairs and mess about, some are into fraud and all types of things that are unacceptable to Christ. But the problem is not so much that non-Christians do these things, it's that Christians just 'tut' and condemn them, refusing to try and help them come to Christ. Just because non-Christians don't live up to Jesus' standards, it doesn't mean that we should have nothing to do with them. Where is the love of God in that? On the contrary, while what they do should never affect our stand with God, our stand with God should most definitely affect them. Being salt and light is our God-given responsibility and mandate and we must never shrink back from it.

Secondly, Jesus himself said that we must be 'in' the world but not 'of' the world. The reason that God puts us bang in the middle of difficult environments is so that we can bring his presence into the situation and effect change by living the Christian life 'in the world'. It's exactly what Jesus meant when he said, 'Go into all your world' and be 'the light of the world'. This is not saying that we should impose our standards on people who don't believe what we believe—there is quite a lot wrong with that. What it is saying is that there really is nowhere on earth, either on the map or in the heart and soul, that is too hard for God. God would have helped Rosie if she hadn't quit, and he will help us too. With God nothing is too difficult. So hang in there. His grace really is sufficient to see you through.

You'll never win if you don't begin

Thirdly, if Rosie was living proof that quitters never win, she was also proof of something even worse: some people quit before they've even begun! It is true that she had started work, but as soon as she realised what she was actually up against she gave up. This is arguably the worse kind of quitting, and makes for some of life's biggest losers. After weighing things up, they conclude that the task ahead is far too big and just isn't worth it.

Now it doesn't have to be like this. You can decide

right now not to be a quitter. Don't let the giant Cowardice in, and don't let its partner Self-deception in either. Most of that stuff about 'it will all be too much' is a bare-faced lie! Take your stand, not by pulling out, but by deciding to shine for Jesus bravely and with complete integrity. And remember, the darker the place the brighter the light will shine; indeed, 'Where sin abounds, grace abounds much more.'

Once you've begun

As sure as eggs is eggs, and no matter how big or small your task, the notion of quitting will sooner or later occur to you. It's human nature. Now it's true that largely thanks to parental influence some people are better equipped to stick at things than others. They've been told since they were very small that if a thing is worth doing, it's worth doing well; and that finishing right is as important as starting right. But even so, the notion of giving up on the task in hand will occur to everyone some time, and if it succeeds once, it may succeed a second and a third . . . and a tenth . . . and a twentieth time. By then, starting a nice bright new task and giving up on it will have become a well-entrenched habit; and Quit will have become a giant of rather unmanageable proportions.

Giant Quit is really another sneaky member of the dirty tricks brigade, because unlike its name this giant doesn't itself give up easily at all. If you're the kind of person who has given up once, this giant will think it can come back again—and again! It won't stop at anything less than God himself. If the last approach didn't work, it will try another one, whether it is the downright negative approach or the spiritual approach or the subtle approach, or the common-sense approach. If these don't work, it will put the frighteners on you with the scare-you-to-death approach. It doesn't matter as long as it gets results—as long as it gets you to quit.

Sometimes, giant Quit will even come up with nice, plausible opt-out clauses. The most classic of these is, 'God has told you to do something else now.' If you've ever wondered if such a statement might be true, just ask yourself this: 'Did Jesus ever say it?' Most emphatically no! The devil is having us on if he tells us that this was God's way. Jesus didn't quit, even when he could have done, even right at the end. He knew very well that God did not want him to do something else now. God wanted to save the human race through him, even if it meant taking those horrific final steps that led through the crucifixion, so 'he stedfastly set his face to go to Jerusalem' (Lk 9:51 AV).

God rarely changes his mind. Rather, people change what God says because it's become hard-going and become a little tough! So if you are ever tempted to throw in the towel, test it out. Ask yourself, What would Jesus do? You may well find that the notion of quitting proves to be pure nonsense.

More sneaky manoeuvres

Giant Quit is so sneaky it will even find certain verses of Scripture (or things that sound like Scripture) to back up its argument. 'Quit,' it says, 'for the battle belongs to the Lord' (not you!). 'Quit,' it repeats. 'Your family comes first.' 'Quit,' it shouts, 'for the honour and glory belong to God' (not a worm like you, so humble yourself and stop trying). But what this giant never tells you is that it's also a malevolent distorter, taking the Scriptures completely out of context.

Giant Quit is also an expert at choosing the best moment in time to get at you. Does it say 'Quit!' when you've just won a battle and are now steaming ahead? Not at all. It waits until you reach another hurdle, when you are feeling disillusioned, discouraged and disappointed. Then, when you're most vulnerable, it comes in for the kill. 'This is hopeless,' it says. 'Quit while you're ahead. Cut your losses and get out now.' But don't believe a word of it. Grit your teeth, hang in there; for the One who has called you is faithful and will bring it to pass.

Nathan's story

My eldest son Nathan hadn't been at school long when, as proud parents, we attended the school's first open day for his class. We were so pleased as we sat before the teacher on the tiny little classroom chairs. She was telling us what a lovely boy Nathan was. For five-and-a-half, 'He's so well-mannered,' she said, 'and so friendly. In fact, he's a model pupil. A real joy to have around.'

I looked at Helen and positively glowed. 'That's my boy!'

The teacher was now looking particularly sympathetic. 'The only problem is,' she continued, 'I'm afraid he's not the cleverest of children. I mean, you probably already know that in fact, academically, he is well behind every other child in his class. He really does find it difficult to concentrate and grasp things. However, he does try hard,' she added, trying to soften the blow. 'But I think he'd benefit from some special needs assistance.'

I can't tell you how we felt. I know we live in a politically correct society where kids with different learning abilities are not to be disparaged in any way, but it was no good; my heart still sank at the thought of the difficulties he might have to overcome. My smile faded. 'Wait till I get him home,' I said. I really felt like laying hands on him there and then, but it wouldn't have been James 5 style—if you know what I mean. Poor mite, it was hardly his fault. 'OK,' I said, 'we'll do everything we can to help him. We'll work with him every night!'

We began at home that very night. We started, gently enough, by counting from one to twelve. Nathan's only problem was that he kept missing out the number ten. The first time this happened, I thought I had misheard; but no, there it was again.

'No, Nathan, it's eight, nine, *ten*, eleven.' But the more we tried the more he omitted it.

Then I thought that if I could get him to remember something that rhymed with ten then this would help him to include the missing number.

'Now look, Nathan,' I suggested, 'it's really very easy. When you get to nine, try and think about a hen, because hen rhymes with ten and ten comes after nine. Eight, nine, think hen, TEN, eleven, twelve.'

'I've got it, Dad,' he said. So we tried again. And I listened with bated breath, hanging on to his every word . . .

He started so confidently: 'One, two, three, four, five, six, seven, eight, nine, chickens . . . !'

'Helen, I give up,' I exclaimed as I threw my hands

in the air. 'This is hopeless! What on earth are we going to do?'

Well of course there wasn't much we could do as far as teaching him was concerned—the teachers were far better at that than we were! But giant Quit wasn't going to win that easily. We decided instead that the best thing to do was to pray with the lad. So for the next six months or so, we laid hands on him every morning before he went to school, praying with him and over him, asking God to impart knowledge and help him with his daily school work.

Two terms later there we were again, sat on those same funny little chairs in front of the same teacher. And this time she wasn't just smiling benignly, she was positively beaming.

'Well, congratulations!' she said. 'I don't know how you've done it but he's really improved. In fact, Nathan's gone from being at the bottom of the class to being in the top three. I'm so impressed,' she continued. 'You must have worked so hard.'

I had to tell her the truth. 'Actually,' I said, 'I did try, but it was useless. He didn't have a clue and neither did I. So it all came to a bit of an abrupt end. Instead, we prayed with him every day that God would impart knowledge and help him to remember it. So I guess the credit really must go to God, not us.'

She laughed as she said, tongue in cheek, 'That's amazing. I don't suppose you'd pray for some more of the little angels, would you?'

I am glad Nathan never gave up and I am certainly glad we didn't give up praying for him. One thing is for sure: God didn't give up on him. It's amazing what can happen if you battle on and refuse to give in.

The DIS giant

Earlier in this chapter I mentioned how giant Quit always strikes when we are at our most vulnerable—discouraged, disillusioned and disappointed. Well, have you ever noticed how the devil is the virtuoso of the DIS word? In Chapter 2 we noted how he is the master of DISguise but there is a whole host of other DIS words and emotions that he uses to try and make us quit. For example, dismay, discontent, distress, discord, disarray, disadvantage, dissatisfaction, disaster, discomfort, discredit, disdain, disease, disgrace, disharmony—the list goes on. More than anyone else, the devil wants you never to win through in God, and he uses giant Quit and all the DIS words he can muster to beat you into giving up.

Fight fire with fire

When you seem to be beset with DIS feelings, recall that there are some other words that begin with DIS with which you can very positively fight off those first negative feelings—words such as disarm, discover, distinguish, discipline, discuss and dismiss, to name but a few. Just don't let the negative DIS's get to you. Keep on keeping on, and you will get there. Make a positive decision never to let a problem or an obstacle become an excuse and your opt-out ticket. And never ever allow a disappointing experience to be the only thing that shapes your future.

Always remember: for every obstacle there is a way over, under, around or through!

A tricky trio

In getting you to quit, the devil also employs a giant trio we'll meet more fully in Chapter 10—giants Ease, Comfort-zone and You-deserve-it. These are the tricksters who tell you that you can stop now, that you deserve a break, a sit down, and a rest. They'll even tell you this before you've begun! 'You've been working so hard recently,' they croon. 'Don't trouble yourself with this too or you'll give yourself a hernia. Put your feet up, have a hot drink, take a nap, take it easy. Nobody cares anyhow, and you'll get no thanks for it.'

If it's not one it's another

If these giants don't get you, along will come another one! Giant Fear, for example, is extremely effective when it comes to getting people to quit. Look the word up in a thesaurus and you'll find every synonym is associated with quitting (and we all know these feelings!). Fear makes us 'cower' from the prospect, 'cringe' from adverse remarks, 'blanch' at the apparent size of the task, 'quail' at the thought of the energy required, 'shrink' from starting, 'tremble' at the unknown, and a host of other things. But do not be put off! Whatever the devil throws at you, whatever you're going through—you don't have to quit.

Colin's story

Colin was a student and member of our church whom I first met while I was a minister in his church. One day he came to see me. It was easy to see he was quite anxious and struggling with something.

Colin's course was in engineering, and his problem was that he was finding it really hard going—almost too hard to cope. To make matters worse the people in his department seemed to be absolutely set against him in one way or another, and Colin was beginning to think he just wouldn't get his degree. What he didn't realise was that he had giant Quit standing in front of him like a bouncer outside an exclusive club. The giant was telling him in no uncertain terms that there was no way through, that he would never get his degree and that he should give up now.

However, when Colin and I really talked about it, it was clear that one of the main things he needed was what many, many of us need at such times—someone to encourage him. As a little boy once said to his minister somewhat pensively, 'Well, I do believe in God but I wish today he was a God with skin on.' Like that little boy, Colin had some faith otherwise he wouldn't have been talking to me. But his faith needed to be bolstered by 'God with skin on'. In other words, God's message of encouragement for Colin needed to come through another person.

Some practical encouragement was required, so I did my best. First, I prayed with him about his studies, and his own strength and courage to keep on with the course. Then a little time later we went into his department to pray there. We often talked about ways of tackling the work and how he could just keep on keeping on. It didn't happen overnight but, little by little, giant Quit was being pushed back, and then back a bit more and then back still further, until it was more or less out of sight. You see, encouragement really does bring the best out in people.

Five years later I had left the area, and one day I was pleased to receive a letter from Colin. Enclosed was his business card—with the following qualifications: BEng, PhD, CEng, MiMechE, MSAE. It looked as if giant Quit had never halted his academic studies. Praise God! This is what Colin wrote:

> I would never have received most of these qualifications if it wasn't for you telling me to 'hang in there' and praying with me and in my department. Of course, the letters after my name are insignificant in God's eyes—the only thing that counts is that our names are written in the Lamb's Book of Life and that we're God's children. However, in the world's eyes they seem to make a difference; they have been a 'ticket' to take me all around the world to places that others can't easily go . . . Through visits to China I've met top government officials, university professors, etc. It's been a privilege. In October, I have my first student coming from Shanghai to do his PhD under my supervision . . . What an opportunity to share with him.
>
> You had a 'word' for me at a house group in 1987: 'You shall be the head and not the tail.' This is happening in a miraculous way. Phil, please, please continue to tell people to 'hang on in there' when they want to quit.

You see, hanging in there really does pay high dividends.

When you decide to win and not to quit, it's like making your own private commitment to God and to yourself. In all likelihood, you also make a public commitment too. In fact, you take a very big step. It's not an easy decision and requires real guts however great or small the task is. So be encouraged. God is with you. For Rosie, for Colin, for you and for me, the important thing is to take that step and stick to it, whatever it takes and however many new ways you have to find of doing so.

You see, winners never quit, and you're a winner. If you want to keep on winning you mustn't quit. We are here to act and to bring about the purposes of God in our generation. So make a positive decision to be the winner God made you and refuse to abandon the task in hand.

What to do in the in-between times

Now there is always a time between God setting out his purposes for you and their actual coming about. This 'in-between time' is crucial. It's not unlike having a baby in that there is an appropriate gestation period, during which you have to wait for growth to happen. In other situations, however, these are often such long, frustrating periods that people describe them as the 'wilderness years'.

During such times, life can be humdrum, frustrating and indeed very difficult. Soon, the giants begin to gather forces to see if they can find a way in. Will it be giant Negativity that succeeds? Or Guilt, or Greed, or Jealousy, or Doubt, or even the giant Corporate? They are ever lurking in the shadows, waiting for an opportunity to start cranking up their engine.

It was during the in-between times that the children of Israel messed up. You will recall they left Egypt and put slavery behind them. God had promised them Canaan—the Promised Land—but it wasn't happening quickly enough for them so they started doubting and moaning and disbelieving God. In the end they even wanted to choose a new leader and go back to Egypt! Psalm 78:40 tells us that in doing so, they 'grieved him in the desert'. We today need to do all we can to keep believing God in those all-important in-between times. Our job is not to grieve but to believe, even when nothing seems to be happening. In fact, there is plenty we can do to help.

Keep the faith

First, keep believing and developing your faith. 'Stand firm' (1 Cor 15:58), and remember that 'Faith comes by hearing, *and hearing* by the word of God' (Rom 10:17). When things don't seem to be going right and you are getting a few knocks, don't panic. In a strange way, failing at times is all part of the learning and winning curve. Just keep on keeping on, and develop your faith through the word of God. It's the only way. 'Let the word of Christ dwell in you richly' (Col 3:16).

Prayer

Secondly, keep praying even when you don't feel like it. Many people feel they have to be spiritually on top in order to pray. It's amazing, but when things are hard or dull, they stop praying because they lack confidence in the presence of God. But don't stop! Remember, as the apostle Paul says, 'We are hard pressed on every side, yet not crushed; we are perplexed, but not in despair; persecuted but not forsaken; struck down, but not destroyed' (2 Cor 4:8–9). With this attitude it is possible to pray at all times—especially when they're tough and apparently barren.

Don't give way in what you say

Thirdly, watch your tongue. Guard your confession. Don't keep saying how awful life is, or you will start to convince yourself. Don't grieve God. Believe him in those wilderness times. Speak positively and not negatively; speak faith and not doubt. Speak the word of God, and hang around people who are full of faith and who will encourage you in your task.

Occupy yourself

Fourthly, keep busy, 'always abounding in the work of the Lord, knowing that your toil is not in vain in the Lord' (1 Cor 15:58) Do you suppose Swan and Edison would have invented the light bulb if they had quit in their nineteenth year of trying, when plenty of people were telling them to call a halt? Thank goodness for their twentieth year! Do you suppose the apostle Paul would have had the influence he did if he'd decided Corinth was a bit much and Ephesus was out of the question? To keep busy for God is one of the best courses we can take when things seem to be dormant. Before we know it we will have made a great achievement for God and for ourselves. So having done all stand, work on and see the salvation of your God.

Start all over again

Finally, don't stay down when you fall. Keep getting back up. Don't stop trying in trying times! Over the years, I have learned three things about failure that giant Quit desperately tries to keep a secret, and they're these: first, failure itself will always quit in the face of persistence; secondly, failure is never a person; and thirdly, failure is never permanent. As Fred Astaire and Ginger Rogers sang in *Swing Time*, it's really important to 'pick yourself up, dust yourself off and start all over again'. The plain truth is, today's successes are often yesterday's failures. So just do it over again. Success without conflict is absolutely unrealistic, but with God you never lose; you just keep practising until you win.

For those who have already quit

I've got one thing to say to you. Get back in the race! It's never too late. God can and will give you a fresh start and another chance. It's time to turn over the old page and start afresh. You have nothing to lose but your giants. Jesus said, 'No man, having put his hand to the plow and looking back, is fit for the kingdom of God' (Lk 9:62). So put your past disappointments, hurts and frustrations behind you and put your trust in God again.

As for me

A rather ironic instance of my own giants at the moment are the ones telling me I can't write this book! Giant Quit is telling me to quit before I make a total fool of myself. Its pals, too, never stop their constant blabber. They are telling me I haven't got time, I've got writer's block, all I'm doing is displaying my inability to express myself, and I'll never finish it. Well, OK, so it's taken me a little longer than I thought but I can't run my life listening to those guys. They're talking absolute rubbish. By the time you read this, those giants will be dead and gone and I'll be ecstatic. Because while the giants roar their heads off (and they can be intimidating enough, I know!) God does give us the victory if we stick with him. And if he can do it for me, believe me, he'll do it for you too. Just keep on going—you're nearly there!

10

What Stops Us Setting Goals?

If you've made that major decision not to quit God's purposes under any circumstances, you'll be aiming for something really important for you and the people around you. Like an athlete, you will be determined to finish the race well, ahead of time if possible. Constantly looking back to see if anyone is catching up, however, is hardly the way that runners win; and if you are going to be a winner, then you too must develop such clear goals that distraction or obstructions can be ignored. Winners need to see ahead, not behind, and they need the goals and the discipline to do just that.

The next two chapters will therefore be devoted to two final sets of nails in the coffins of our giants! First, we'll look at what can still make us look back and prevent us setting goals. Secondly, we'll look at how to deal with such obstacles, and go forward. Naturally, as we have already seen, we will first need to find out exactly what God wants for us; but we also need to set realistic, achievable goals to get the job done.

Wandering aimlessly

I suppose we all know people who get out of bed each day and have no plans beyond the cornflake packet.

These people never make much of a difference and are rarely effective; they lose far more often than they win. How true the saying is that 'when we fail to plan, we simply plan to fail'. Bobby Knight, the head basketball coach for Indiana University, led his team to victory in no fewer than three national championships, so he must know something about what it takes to win through. He said, 'The will to win is nothing without the will to prepare to win.'

Many, many people have a worthy dream or vision from God, but they fail in their dream, not from a lack of gifts or talent, or even commitment or resources— but from not having a serious, effective strategy. The experts tell us that goal-making and goal-achieving are indeed so demanding that a massive 97 per cent of people in our society today do not have any organised goals programme.

Now if this is true, the chances are you're one of them! Some folk approach life with a *que sera sera* attitude—what will be, will be. Others, more laudably perhaps, think they can achieve their dreams through sheer hard work. But while there is no substitute for working hard, the need is not to work harder but to work smarter (and end up less shattered every day!). Working smarter makes sense, as does overcoming every giant that gets in the way, but how do you do that without setting achievable goals? Having God-oriented goals is essential.

The goals we need will affect our personal, family, spiritual and church lives; our careers, leadership, ministry, finances and even fitness. By making an irreversible decision to be a goal-setter and a goal-achiever, doing today what most people won't, you will undoubtedly secure having tomorrow what most people can't. So may I suggest that if you haven't got any goals, your first goal should be to set some?

The good thing is, all giants do really badly in the face of systematic, effective goal-setting. When someone takes time out to set specific goals in God, and is determined to pray and see them through, that person will be within reach of monumental change—and serious progress is going to be made against the giants' throttling hold.

But if goal-setting is so effective, why is it that only 3 per cent of people ever bother to have a balanced goal programme? The experts tell us there are five main reasons why this is the case:

- Fear
- Low self-esteem
- Lack of understanding
- Unwillingness to make the time
- Inability to put a goal strategy together

Let us now look at these more closely.

Reason no. 1—fear

Many people never set realistic goals because of fear. Most fear, of course, turns out to be largely unfounded, but does that stop us being struck with worry and dread? It does not. Of course, when we handle fear well, we do make headway. But when fear becomes a giant, it inhibits, menaces and immobilises us more successfully than any other giant. Fear is the master tutor in the art of producing so-called qualified, rational excuses, and the university it works from awards degrees in cowardice and procrastination.

Giant Fear normally strings its lectures along with

phrases like 'If only you had . . . but you haven't. What a disaster!' and 'What if this happens? . . . watch out!' If only you had time . . . if only you had youth on your side . . . if only you'd had a good start . . . if only you had the right contacts; what if you die . . . what if there's no money . . . what if you can't . . .?' At this point, an interesting thing often begins to happen: the doubts of the mind—all quite valuable in their own way for making you think things through—sneakily drop to become doubts of the heart. And doubts of the heart are not useful at all. They destroy individuals, groups and even whole nations.

So when giant Fear plants 'if only . . . watch out' thoughts in you, take care! They can grow out of control, carefully cultivated and nurtured by the most amazing lies from the devil's compost heap. These plants can take over, and the garden of your life can have a solid bed of deep-rooted, prize-winning fears in it. Like couch grass in the soil, Fear's truthless roots will burrow deep down into the recesses of your mind and spirit where they are difficult to locate and still more difficult to eliminate. Then, just when you feel it is safe to venture out and take a step of faith, you're stuck. Fear dictates your every move, aiming to choke the very faith and life of God out of you. Napoleon Hill, in his book *Think and Grow Rich*, eloquently says:

Fear paralyses the faculty of reason, destroys the faculty of imagination, kills off self-reliance, undermines enthusiasm, encourages procrastination and makes self-control an impossibility. It takes the charm from one's personality, destroys the possibility of accurate thinking, diverts concentration and effort: it masters persistence, turns willpower into nothingness, destroys ambition, beclouds the memory, and invites failure in every conceivable form: it kills love, and assassinates the finer emotions of the heart, discourages friendship, and invites disaster in a hundred different forms, leading to sleeplessness, misery and unhappiness. . . .

In short, giant Fear is the ultimate personality-suppressor and determined dream-killer. It is also, beyond doubt, the best preventer of goal-setting that could ever have been devised.

Name that fear

To punch the giant Fear in the belly, however, is never as hard as it sounds. Believe it or not, all it needs is just a tiny pinprick of truth-telling. Just take courage from God, name your fear, and ask yourself 'Is this true?' I guarantee that in naming it and asking that question, you'll find the fear you've named is almost always a lie!

Personal experience

The main key to eliminating fears, however, is undoubtedly to fix your eyes on Jesus. As you develop your daily relationship with him, you will find that his love really does cast out fear.

There have been times when Helen and I have been so haunted by the giants Lack and Fear that we haven't known what to do. Perhaps a number of unexpected bills have come in and we just haven't had any way of paying them. We would put them aside, only a few days later to receive the final demand, always in red, and always, it seemed, on the same day that the bank manager wrote to remind us we were overdrawn!

At precisely these moments, Fear would start whispering, 'If only you had . . .' followed by 'What if this?' and 'What if that?' We'd get so wound up into a right old frenzy that it would cause sleeplessness, irritability, nausea, and a host of other side effects. We've seen this frenzy happen to whole churches, and to other leaders too—so beware!

The fascinating thing is that whenever Helen and I have then spent some serious time waiting on God through prayer and fasting and absorbing his word, God really has broken through. It's as if faith has walked in, and doubt and fear have had to make a sharp exit. And strangely, although the problem was still the same, we would change. Our faith levels would rise up high, our spirits would become strong, and if we were careful to do exactly what God told us and put our total trust in him, he'd come to the rescue just at the right time—every time. He has never let us down, and nor will he let you down, for 'those who wait upon the Lord shall have renewed strength' (Is 40:31).

Decide to have direction

Another thing we can do to address Fear is to realise that clear direction always helps. Think of someone travelling to the capital city by car for the first time for a very important meeting. Driving on their own from one end of the city to the other during the rush hour, with no directions or map, will understandably cause fear and worry. Everyone knows the capital is a hopeless place to get around if you don't know it. What's more, you're bound to turn up late—through getting lost and having to continually stop and ask the way.

However, if the same person has good directions,

an up-to-date map, and a good navigator, fear and worry would largely disappear. In such circumstances, the capital is not so difficult a place to get around. The chances are he or she will arrive on time, perhaps even with some minutes to spare, to relax and get in the right frame of mind for that all-important appointment.

You see, clear direction and knowing exactly where you are going definitely goes a long way in dealing with Fear. Of course, this brings us back to the whole business of coming up with a clear goal strategy. Zig Ziglar in his book *Over the Top* says,

> Unfortunately very few people are equipped with specific directions on how to navigate the highways of life. No wonder the overwhelming majority of people end up at the end of life's journey with just a fraction of what life has to offer.

Few people would argue with this, nor with the fact that people who have clear direction and goals in their lives go much further and faster, achieving so much more in all areas of life, than those who don't.

So you really can defeat giant Fear in your life, whatever form it takes. First, name your fears and tell yourself the truth about them; secondly, spend time with God and develop your relationship with him; and lastly, know precisely where you are going by setting bite-sized, achievable goals in your day-to-day life. To gain any ground at all, beating giant Fear must be a top priority.

Just one final note about fear. Whatever you do, don't allow the fear and pain of past disappointments to haunt you and stop you having a new goals programme. Giant Disappointment can prove to be a real immobiliser.

Just because you've set goals in the past and were disappointed when you didn't achieve them, is no good reason for not setting new and fresh goals today. Remember—to hit 50–60 per cent or 70 per cent of your God-given goal is better than hitting 100 per cent of nothing.

To accomplish your new goals remember these four steps: plan purposefully, prepare prayerfully, proceed positively and pursue persistently. If you follow this simple four-step strategy you will be well on your way to achieving, believe me! Whoever it was who said, 'Only those who dare to fail greatly can ever achieve greatly' was absolutely spot on. So lay your past disappointments to rest once and for all and set a few new goals. You've got nothing to lose and every-thing to gain. Go for it!

Reason no. 2—low self-esteem

A second barrier to setting specific personal goals is low self-esteem. Although everyone has seeds of greatness in them and is capable of phenomenal achievement, many people also have an underlying mindset of worthlessness, inferiority and low self-opinion. It may be that their circumstances have somehow persuaded them not to set goals; or they may think they'd never achieve any goal, however small; or they may be seriously affected by the Not Me giant we spoke about in Chapter 8. But just where do these titanic inadequacies come from? How are they conceived? Where are they birthed?

Cue yet another ugly giant by the name of Labeller!

You may well have come across this one already. In fact, I am sure it has introduced itself to you on more than one occasion. It's very pushy, and very vocal, and it never lets an opportunity slip by. Its sole objective is to attach negative labels of such weight and pseudo-authority that they can both cripple and paralyse, in time rendering a person totally ineffective and next to useless.

Alec

In one church where I was minister there was a young man whom we will call Alec. I remember him as being nervous, insecure, slightly immature—the over-mothered type. He was unemployed and his demeanour at that particular time would never encourage any employer to give him a job.

However, Alec was talented in many ways and I wanted to bring out his maximum potential so that he could be blessed and become a blessing to others as well. For instance, he played the guitar reasonably well, but he always declined playing it in public, saying, 'I couldn't possibly do that. I'm just not up to it.'

I tried all sorts of tacks. 'Hey, Alec! What about giving a five-minute testimony at the house group in three weeks' time?' It was a small group and by giving him plenty of time to prepare and get used to the idea I thought he might bite. Unfortunately I got the same old reply.

'What about if I asked you some questions? Would that be easier?'

'Er, I don't think so. I'll make a mess of it. Thanks, Pastor, but no thanks.'

Not easily deterred, a couple of weeks later I tried

again: 'Alec, would you do me a great big favour?
One of the guys who normally passes around the
offering plates is on holiday on Sunday; would you
fill in for him?'

'What would I have to do, Pastor?' he asked.

'Well, during a hymn you would pass the offering
plate around one side of the church. Then you'd come
to the front of the church and place the plate on the
table and then sit down again. It's as simple as that.
There's nothing to it.'

He looked at me, thinking long and hard. After
quite a while he said, 'Sorry, Pastor, I don't think
I'm up to it. I'll give it a miss, if it's all the same to
you.'

And so it went on. Whatever I asked him to do—
give the books out, welcome people at the door, talk
to someone, help clean the church, push a few leaflets
through letter boxes, sell ice cream at a church function—he would always say, 'I don't want to let you
down, Pastor. Perhaps some other time.' I couldn't
understand it. It wasn't as if he wasn't capable. He
was! There was obviously some hidden agenda here. I
decided the only thing was to get alongside him and
try to find out where the real problem lay.

Slowly, Alec did begin to open up. He was an only
son and like most kids he'd absolutely adored his
father. They'd laughed together, and gone fishing
together; they'd done homework together and talked
over all those awkward questions together that all
little boys ask. On sports day, Dad always managed
to get time off work—there he'd been on the sidelines,
cheering and urging Alec on. It had been Dad who
bought him his first guitar, and taught him to play
simple chords. It had been Dad who taught him to

ride his bike. Dad had always been there and, in short, Dad had been Alec's hero.

Then suddenly, when Alec was about twelve, his father had had a heart attack and died. Alec was absolutely devastated. Dad was gone and the bottom had fallen out of Alec's world. No matter what his mother did (or anybody else for that matter) it didn't help. He was inconsolable.

Alec took the next six months off school. When he finally did go back, he found himself well behind the rest of the class. He was still trying to come to terms with the death of his father, and he found he couldn't concentrate. As time went by, it was becoming obvious that even his teacher was getting more and more frustrated at Alec's lack of progress.

Enter giant Labeller, who spoke through the rest of the kids in the class. (Giants just love finding someone to fire their bullets and do their yelling for them!) 'Dunce,' the other kids would retort. 'Thicko', 'Idiot', 'Useless', 'Wimp', 'Dumbo', 'Weakling', 'Birdbrain'. Alec was soon the laughing stock and the butt of everybody's jokes.

Sadly, giant Labeller often uses the mouths of children. School pupils can be particularly ruthless and vicious in what they have to say, and the school playground is often the anvil where the devil forges life-destroying labels. Labeller had now started on Alec in earnest, supergluing and riveting a number of labels onto him, classifying him as 'different', 'odd', 'inferior', 'unacceptable', 'rejected', and 'lonely'. The giant was having a party doing what it does best—squeezing the very life and personality out of someone, robbing him of his true potential and rendering him totally inadequate.

Then, to finish the job off completely, Labeller looked to see who else it could use. Its attention turned to the teacher, and to help things along it summoned the services of another giant, Frustration (sometimes known as The Exasperator). Between them they concocted a lethal cocktail for finally ridding Alec of any self-respect and self-worth, and one day, from sheer exasperation, the teacher did blow up. In view of the whole class, this teacher bellowed at the top of his voice, 'You're useless! What's the matter with you, boy? Are you stupid? Everything you do ends up wrong! You will never amount to anything! Did you hear me? You are a waster! Now get out of my sight!'

Frustration had done its job horribly well. Every word penetrated the bull's-eye of Alec's heart. Labeller moved in for the kill with a final onslaught intended to cause irreversible harm and setback; it had a field day pinning on multi-coloured, psychedelic labels that yelled, 'worthless', 'hopeless', 'useless', 'failure', 'waster', 'disappointment', 'second class', 'subordinate', 'unworthy', 'unacceptable', and 'not good enough'.

By the time I knew him, Alec honestly believed that he was useless—someone who would never amount to anything. It was the self-fulfilling prophecy again. If you label people unkindly long enough, they may become those labels. This is why I could never get Alec to do anything in church.

Of course, Labeller is a liar. It's an exemplar of the straight face, the con-person extraordinaire, and it's amazingly good at making you believe its lies. But it does so because it knows you'll never set goals and win through if you think you're useless and worth nothing. That's why it pins labels on you that say loser, wimp, depressant, bad husband, bad wife, lousy parent, idle, inferior, average, fat, thin, black, unsociable, weak, sick, poor, ugly, pathetic, victim, useless . . . the list is endless.

God's remedy

However, Labeller is not the only player here. We have seen before that fighting fire with fire can be extremely effective, and the truth is that God also attaches labels to you—positive, affirming labels of self-worth and self-esteem. From the beginning of creation God has given us labels such as winner, new creation, successful, forgiven, achiever, loved, unique, priceless, child of God, victorious, righteous, creative, precious, gifted, heaven-bound, special and so on. There is an endless reservoir of positive labels that is provided for each one of us by Almighty God.

Take time to search the Scriptures and find out for yourself who you really are in Christ. Let God speak to you and tell you how passionately he loves you— yes, you! Realise that you really are a winner and that in God you can achieve absolutely anything. There need be no fear of failure and you need have no problems whatsoever in setting yourself worthwhile goals and achieving them.

Now I know what you're asking: 'What became of Alec?' Well, all I could do was to keep spending time with him, reinforcing his worth and who he was in Christ. I constantly tried to build him up, telling him that he was a winner and that in God he could really make something of his life. I helped him to set some personal achievable goals which eventually he managed to attain. Many years later, I believe his relationship with God is still growing, but the story illustrates how powerful the giant Labeller can be and just what type of hold those labels can have over us until we face them and reject them.

As I tell you the story of Alec, I'm not finding it easy. In fact it is difficult to explain some of the emotions I do feel. I feel angry and upset. I've wanted to weep when thinking about the adverse effect labels have on untold millions every day. Perhaps it is because I recognise some of the labels that Labeller has stuck on me over the years. I'd love to get hold of this giant and throttle the life out of it. I hate it. Giant Labeller is a liar, a deceiver and an absolute scum bag!

But getting hold of Labeller is difficult. It's a sly old fox. It always hides behind someone else. Although a giant, it's not big enough to do its own dirty work: which suddenly makes me pull up short. How many times in the past have I partnered Labeller and been a willing accomplice? How many people have I unjustly labelled through the words I have spoken and the things I have done, even if sometimes it was in jest? Labeller's most powerful accomplices are unsuspecting folk like you and me. It makes me even more determined from now on to do all I can to build up, motivate and inspire people to reach their fullest potential—to be exactly who God created them to be.

I also guess that you now have an insight into why I wanted to write such a book as this in the first place. I just want to tell you that you're a winner! So be encouraged and decide to have goals; go for it with everything you've got. You can do it. You've got what it takes. Few people escape the scathing attacks of Labeller, but this one thing I do know: Greater is he that is in you, than the Labeller that's in the world.

Reason no. 3—lack of understanding

Experts in the field of strategy planning also conclude that a third reason we are poor goal-setters and goal-achievers is that we lack the basic understanding of the real long-term benefits. In order to progress a little further down this line, think about the following four questions:

1. What does God want me to achieve?
2. What do I really believe I have to do to bring it about and get there?
3. How many steps will it take?
4. What exactly are they?

It should go without saying that if you discipline yourself to be diligent in 2, 3 and 4, then you should be able eventually to achieve 1—your final objective. And believe me, the long-term benefits of doing what God wants you to achieve are a million times better than not doing it.

Maybe you're thinking that this is fine for those who haven't got much to do and have plenty of time on their hands, but you are simply too busy. You already work fourteen hours a day six-and-a-half days a week. Where on earth are you going to find the extra time for putting a goals programme together?

Well, this leads me nicely to the next reason why the majority of people never set goals, so read on.

Reason no. 4—unwillingness to make the time

It's true that developing a personal, effective goals programme takes time. It could take ten, twenty or even more hours initially to put a goals strategy together for yourself, and in all probability you think you just haven't got that sort of time on your hands. Lack of time has always been, and will always be, a major problem. It was William Penn who said, 'Time is what we want most, but what alas we use worst.'

However, each day has the same number of hours in it for everyone. It is just that some people get the best out of their time and others waste it. Have you watched no television at all in the last week? Have you made no journeys that you didn't absolutely have to make, that someone else might have made for you? The plain truth is, each one of us finds time to do what we think is important and urgent. The basic problem is not the lack of time, but the lack of direction.

Taking the long-term view

Are you really saving time long term by taking things as they come? This is miserably short-term behaviour. The long-term view says that by investing the time it takes to set up such a programme, it could well save and therefore create for you between an extra five and ten hours of valuable, productive time every week! Doesn't it actually make more sense to take the long-term view? Make that decision to start—it really is half the battle won. One thing is for sure: without any action there is never going to be any real progress; if you really want to reach God's dream for you, the truth is you *have* to find the time. Remember, the only way you are sure to fail is by not making the effort at all. So start now!

More giants looking your way

At this point you may, unknowingly, have the nicest-looking of all the giants smiling engagingly at you. It's called Ease, and it has a couple of siblings called Comfort-zone and You-deserve-it. These three are almost inseparable, and they always sing in harmony. What happens is this: Ease comes along and says, 'Hey—what are you, a masochist or something? Take it easy.' Comfort-zone says, 'Think of all the hard work you've put in this week. You need a rest.' 'Yeah,' soothes You-deserve-it. 'You deserve it!'

I don't need to go on about Ease, Comfort-zone and You-deserve-it, because we all know them, and we can all recognise them once we take the trouble to look. But giant Ease doesn't want you to do anything so productive as setting goals because it really does not want you to leave your comfort zone, i.e. the status quo, and do that second mile, nor even the first one for that matter. Its dirty game is to prevent you doing any distance at all in the direction of your God-given destiny, and it has a silky sweet way of getting you to thumb a lift in the opposite direction.

Think about it. You have been given this day to use as you will. You can waste it or you can use it for good. What you choose to do with it is important because you are exchanging no less than a day of your life for it. Make it count by being a goal-setter and a goal-pursuer. In the process you will find you will create yourself considerably more time to do the worthwhile things in life.

Reason no. 5—inability to put a goal strategy together

And so to the final reason that experts give us for why the majority of people don't set goals for themselves. It is the inability to put a goals programme together. The truth is, most of us haven't got a clue about the nitty-gritty of effective goal-setting. So the next chapter begins with a successful and achievable formula for setting and achieving those all-important goals.

11

Setting Goals: A Very Practical Weapon

We have seen that, because they have either fears, or low self-esteem, or too little time, or can't see the benefits, or don't know how, a massive 97 per cent of people don't set themselves any goals. But goals are the most important practical weapon you will have against the giants in your life. They will also be the transport that will move you forward with your God-given dreams—a step at a time, in the intended direction.

Make time

In setting goals, one of the first things you need to set aside for yourself is time. *Make* time—you can if you really want to! Why not decide right now to do so? Explain to someone your need and ask if they could make that trip on this occasion; explain your need to the next person on the phone and ask if you could phone them back in a few hours; turn off the TV or the radio; excuse yourself from the meeting; and go to another room with a pen and paper and *start*. You can do it! I promise you that if you do make the effort and find the time to establish a real plan of action through goal-setting, you will unquestionably

have much more time in the future to do what you
need to do.

How goals work—and how they don't!

Goals create motivation, motivation creates energy,
and energy creates the type of activity that make
your dreams a reality. But goals mean precious little
while they are just figments of your imagination. So
first, just brainstorm every goal idea you have, clear
or unclear, big or small. Take a blank sheet of paper
and write down all your thoughts, including what
you are doing about the goals you are currently pursuing and, just as important, what you are not doing.
Notice the gaps between intention and action. Until
you do this, your dreams, hopes and aspirations are
nothing but wandering generalities instead of being
meaningful specifics. Writing it all down says you are
taking goal-setting seriously; it's a very concrete step
to take.

Second, spend some time with God, talking it
through with him. Praise him for the ideas and
inspiration you've had in this brainstorming session.
Praise him, too, for the times when you have already
had the courage and commitment to do what you
believe in him to be right. Confess the gaps in your
actions, saying what they really are, and seek his
guidance and courage to defeat your malingering
giants and get on track.

Committing your goals to paper

OK, so you've done some brainstorming, and you'll
probably have found that there are basically seven

areas of your life into which your thoughts about your goals generally fall. These areas are: physical, family, finance, social, spiritual, intellectual, and work. Now we're going to get down to the real nitty-gritty of goal-setting, and it's more important than ever that you clearly write your goals down because this is when you get specific—no more fudging! The prophet Habakkuk said that God told him to 'write down clearly . . . what I have revealed to you, so that it can be read at a glance' (Hab 2:2)—very wise advice indeed, even if it was given over 2,500 years ago!

Goal-setting principles: ten simple steps

Here are ten simple steps for setting any individual goals. It really doesn't matter what area the goal is in. As long as you follow the steps described below, you should have no problem. Of course, giant Fear would just love to make you think that goal-setting (and achieving, for that matter) is really daunting, but as usual it's just not true! It's not half as difficult as you might think once you get started, and it even gets quite exciting. So for each goal:

1. Earnestly seek God and ask, 'What is it that God wants me to achieve and do?'
2. Clearly identify the goal by writing it down in no more than two sentences.
3. Set a specific deadline for achievement.
4. List all the skills and knowledge required for realising the goal.
5. List all the obstacles or giants you think you will have to overcome to obtain the goal.

6. Identify people in groups you could work with in achieving the goal.

7. Make a plan of action. How many steps will it take? What are they? List them. Can they be broken down into smaller steps? Make sure each step has its own time deadline attached to it.

8. List all the benefits of achieving the goal. This will help you to keep your focus on why realising your goal is so important.

9. Look at and review your goal daily. Determine to bring your goal that little bit nearer to fulfilment each and every day. Determine to see it through and overcome all those giants that have a habit of getting in your way. When you do face the obstacles (and some days will be worse than others), don't change your mind about your goal, just change your direction in order to get there. Do something every day to move towards your goal. Ask God to help you be absolutely relentless and committed in your pursuit.

10. Write down how you are going to celebrate when you finally reach that goal. It's good to celebrate. It gives us something to look forward to. What about a special meal, or a day out; or if it's the church—what about a party?

One thing is for certain: the giants won't be doing any celebrating with you—not even giant Ease and giant You-deserve-it. They simply hate people setting and actually achieving goals; they lied to you in the first place to stop you. When you've reached your first goal, be sure to set yourself another one, following the ten-step strategy once again. Of course, there's no reason why you shouldn't be working on a number of goals at the same time. So set to it.

The measuring rod

Now you've set one or more goals, you'll be amazed at how having them allows you to measure your progress—what, where and how far you have to go to realise God's ultimate purposes for you. The golden maxim to remember here is: if it can't be measured, then it's not a goal (for the truth is, if something can be measured, it can be managed; but if it can't be measured, it will never be managed!).

In my particular job, I talk to a lot of people about goals—especially leaders and those involved in ministry of some kind. Most of them believe they've got goals, but in reality they frequently have nothing more than pipe dreams! Always remember that a goal is a meaningful specific. For example, for a pastor to say, 'Within the next twelve months I want my church to grow as much as possible' is, forgive me, as good as useless. A goal must always be specific: for example, 'Within the next twelve months I want my church to grow by a minimum of thirty-five adults, and this is how I am going to achieve it.' You see, goals must have:

(a) a specific target (thirty-five adults)
(b) a specific strategy (this is how I will achieve it)
(c) a specific deadline (within the next twelve months)

This, of course, is a church example but it's exactly the same whatever sphere the goal is in. Don't deal with generalities—focus on specifics. Wanting 'to help in

Africa' is not a goal. Rather, for example, aim to raise a specific sum, through a community event, at a specific time, for a certain charity involved in Africa. That's a measurable, achievable goal.

Self-deception

Now the giant Self-deception has a particularly slippery part to play when it comes to measuring our progress. It's one of the last giants to leave any scene, because our integrity is in many ways the best thing we have before God. So when you've set your goals, and have begun to measure your progress, do be honest in everything you talk about with God and in everything you tell yourself.

A friend of mine called Frin once did this and came up with a rather unpleasant surprise. She'd been telling herself for years that she was spiritually pretty healthy, and that her goal was to stay that way. But when she wrote down what she actually did, she had to admit that she didn't actually pray very often outside church, or read the Bible for that matter, and that her gifts, when directed to those less fortunate than herself in the community, were frequently less than generous. Were her goals and behaviour matching up? In a word, no!

You too are probably susceptible to kidding yourself from time to time, and you too may not know it. Indeed, the giant Self-deception is one of the few giants that keeps absolutely silent—its entire focus is on making sure you don't notice that you sometimes lie to yourself. Self-deception tells countless students that because they are taking a degree course they are actually studying for that degree (in fact the student in question may be doing no such thing). Self-deception tells you that because you are always thinking about something you are actually making headway on it; and that because a particular thing is locked at the back of your mind (you plan to address it 'at some stage') everything's just hunky-dory. Self-deception is just superb at telling you that because you've got some good ideas you must obviously be doing everything in your power to achieve them.

Sadly, nothing may be further from the truth. Having good ideas doesn't mean you are even remotely working towards them as proper goals. It just means you have some illusions! Specific goals, such as those you have now written down, will require more than thought, and more than talk. You must plan your work and work your plan to achieve them. Achievement is spelled H-A-R-D   W-O-R-K.

Be realistic

So far so good. You've set some specific goals, you'll be able to measure your progress and you'll avoid Self-deception like the plague. Are you also being realistic? It's no good saying at fifty years old, 'I want to be an Olympic gymnast.' Instead, the goal might be to raise money for a brilliant sports facility for local kids who have nowhere to go except the streets, so that maybe one of them might become a top-class gymnast.

In fact, goals that are realistic—as well as clear and measurable—will take you even further. You can be confident of this, because realistic goals help you maintain the right mental attitude and keep your focus on the real target. Oliver Wendell Holmes said,

. . . the great thing in this world is not so much where we stand, but in what direction we are moving. To reach the port of heaven we must sail sometimes with the wind and sometimes against it—but we must sail and not drift nor lie at anchor.

In other words, realistic goals will keep you moving in the right direction.

Two final notes of caution

It is good to have goals for every area of our lives but, as we saw in Chapter 7, we need to make sure that the dreams and goals we have fall in line with God's purposes for our lives. That's the first thing we need to be careful about.

The second is this: we need to ask ourselves, 'Is the goal we're going after worth the cost?' You can go after some goals and in your pursuit neglect the many other areas of your life. Indeed, a sad fact of church life is that some Christian leaders are so devoted to their ministry they neglect their marriages and end up with broken families. The same goes for some people who want to get to the top of their profession—they concentrate so much on their work, impressing the boss and climbing the professional ladder that they neglect other important areas of their lives. It really is no good to climb a particular ladder only to find when we reach the top that it's leaning against the wrong wall!

So be careful to have your priorities right. Don't try to reach one goal, however worthy, which makes you overlook or fail in other areas that could be more important. Jesus was quite clear about this. That's why he said such things as, 'What does it profit a person if he gains the whole world and then loses his soul?' (Mk 8:36).

Keep on keeping on

It's already been said that all kinds of giants will try to get you to quit. But by now, you'll know how not to. You really can be determined to keep on keeping on, with your eyes fixed on Jesus, the author and finisher of your dream. In him, you will most certainly get there and achieve! I appreciate it is not going to be easy. Jesus never said it would be, but he did say it would be worth it. The question we need to ask is: Are we willing to give ourselves whole-heartedly to the goal-making process?

Let me encourage you. I believe you have within you the capacity to reach all your goals. You can do all things through Christ who strengthens you (see Philippians 4:13). You have been born a winner and that means you've definitely got what it takes to make your goals happen. Of course, there are small goals and large goals. There are short-term, inter-mediate and long-term goals. But don't be afraid! Set to it, and see the giants in your life come a-tumblin' down. Emerson was absolutely right when he said, 'What lies behind us, and what lies in front of us, pales into insignificance when compared with what lies within us.'

Even more important than practical weapons

Having goals is an enormous practical weapon when it comes to giant-killing, and just as exciting as it's made out to be. But I don't want to give you the wrong impression. I don't want you to think that having an effective goals programme will defeat all the giants by itself. If you want to move on with God and enter into your full inheritance with Christ, there's more to it than just a goals programme, excellent though that may be.

Back to David

This book has been all about how to handle problems that are so big you can't see beyond them and so stubborn that they keep getting in the way. How big are your giants? One thing is for sure: David's giant was one of the biggest he ever had to face.

The problem David faced is described in 1 Samuel 17. The Israelites were encamped, ready to do battle, on one mountainside above the Valley of Elah. On the other side camped the enemy—the Philistines. The valley between them was the front line. And every single day for about six weeks the militant Israelite army would charge down the mountain towards the enemy forces; but before they could reach the battle line, a Herculean titan of a man called Goliath of Gath swaggered out, and threatened and terrorised the Israelite warriors. The Bible tells us that this menacing, intimidating creature was almost ten feet tall. To make matters worse, he wore a coat of brass that weighed an extra 125lb, and he carried a spear like a weaver's beam.

We are talking about one overpowering guy here. Morning after morning, this Philistine champion would strut across the slopes of the valley, roaring out threats and constantly defying the armies of the living God. You can just imagine his tormenting war-cry echoing around the valley with thundering per-sistence. And every time the Israelites saw or heard this elephantine strong-man, it would strike terror into their hearts and stop them dead in their tracks. And every time they would opt to make a hasty retreat. Not one of them felt equipped to take on the challenge. The Bible tells us that 'Saul and all the Israelites were dismayed and greatly afraid'.

This word 'dismayed' here means they had 'lost all courage'. In their own eyes, they saw themselves as defeated even though they were still encamped on the mountainside. Why? They had their attention focused on the wrong thing! What they were looking at was the giant, and who could blame them? However, what their focus should have been fixed on was not Goliath, but God—the Lord of hosts, the one who could easily have given them victory 'over any giant'.

Enter the slayer

Suddenly a young shepherd boy appeared on the scene—David, the son of Jesse. His father had sent him to the battlefield to take food to his elder brothers who were soldiers in the Israelite army, and also to bring back a report from the commanding officer.

The lad arrived just in time to see Israel pluck up enough courage to storm down into the valley once again; and when he heard the Israelites' battle cry, he no doubt ran to go with them. Totally unarmed, this whipper-snapper raced towards the enemy, shouting greetings to his brothers at the same time. Then, just as every other day, the giant Goliath made his grand entrance and as per usual the Israelite soldiers dispersed in every direction, as fast as they could.

Now David just could not believe the way the Israelites—God's chosen people—allowed themselves to be so intimidated by Goliath. OK, the giant was big, but he was nowhere near a match for the God of all Israel, the covenant-keeping God. However, when David asked about this, all he got was a clip round the ear and a right mouthful.

'What do you know about it anyway?' they said. 'Can't you see the size of him?'

David replied, 'But . . . who is this uncircumcised Philistine that he should defy the armies of the living God?' In other words, it didn't matter how big and intimidating he was, Goliath was a Philistine—unlike the children of Israel who were God's own covenant people. Therefore, David believed the giant didn't stand a chance; he was convinced that the battle belonged to the Lord, who would bring victory, as in fact he told Goliath when he finally met him face to face.

Now David was not stupid. He realised that no human combat and no clever weaponry could win this one. The fight had to be fought with spiritual weapons, in the name of the Lord. In the Spirit, David somehow knew what the apostle Paul knew centuries later: 'The weapons of our warfare are not carnal but are mighty through God, to the pulling down of strongholds' (2 Cor 10:4). This shepherd boy may well have been young, but he nevertheless recognised the need for spiritual weaponry when he saw it. He obviously believed what the prophet Zechariah believed—that 'it's not by might, or by power [manmade weapons] but by my Spirit says the Lord (Zech 4:6).

David applies for the job

So off David went to King Saul, and offered to fight the giant on behalf of Israel. The king almost laughed and you can imagine him saying something like, 'Don't be silly—you're just a lad! Look at him! He's an experienced warrior—just look at the size of him!'

David then shared something of his pedigree and background. He told the king how the Lord had enabled him to fight a lion and a bear on the hillside and kill them both while he was on his own protecting the sheep. He was confident that, just as the Lord had delivered him from the paws of those life-threatening beasts, the same God would deliver him from the hand of this Philistine. You see, even at this young age, David had already proved himself in private. And he believed in God that, because of this private proof, he was now ready for the public arena.

Private battles

This holds an important lesson for us when we too crave the public limelight. If we want to be seen openly as people of power and men and women of God, we will have to win some considerable personal and private battles first. Yes, there are many people who want to be great preachers, to heal the sick and raise the dead, scoring some great public victories. Yet behind the scenes the same people and their family lives may leave a lot to be desired. In some cases they're actually falling apart at the seams. Personal and private victories must always come before public ones. Only when we are faithful in the little and the unseen things of life—in the first mile, as it were—will God give us victory in the more glorious second mile, in the big visible things of the public arena.

Back to the Valley of Elah

In the event, of course, King Saul had no alternative. There were no other takers, so David landed the job. Saul gave him his blessing and offered him his own personal armour, but when David put it on, it buried him! He couldn't move a muscle, let alone kill a giant. How ridiculous this young boy must have looked in Saul's helmet and coat of mail! This just wasn't him, and it didn't feel right. David realised he didn't stand a chance of doing it Saul's way. He was far more at home with a shepherd's sling and a stone or two, and a steadfast trust in his God. David's greatest protection was his inner shield of faith. The thing that kept him cool, confident and composed in the midst of his greatest danger was his unshakeable trust in God.

So David took off Saul's armour and explained that the giant must be defeated God's way, not in human ways. Spiritual weapons were the order of the day, not physical ones.

And history was made

The rest is history. With his sling and a smooth stone and that mighty confidence in the name of the Lord, this young herdsman put an end to the giant's reign of terror once and for all. Goliath was never to rise again to see another day.

So what about your giants?

How big are your giants? Well, it doesn't matter, because they can be beaten and you can most definitely have victory over them. But remember, it will never be through human might or power or persuasion or ability alone; it will have to be 'by my Spirit, says the Lord'.

In other words, our giants are only going to fall and victory will only be ours if in the end we trust God, using all the spiritual weapons he has provided for us. Sadly, many Christians today seem to be turning to worldly methods for dealing with the spiritual problems which invade their lives. But remember Psalm 1: 'Blessed is the person who does not take the counsel of the ungodly.' This doesn't mean that unbelievers don't have certain genuine skills and know-how. What it means is that we must open wide the whole subject of not using worldly methods and weapons for spiritual problems. In the last chapter, therefore, this is exactly what we will concentrate on—how to use the spiritual weapons we have been given by Almighty God.

12

Spiritual Weapons: Slay Your Giant

When I was finishing the previous chapter, I knew that all I had to do now was to put together the last chapter on spiritual weapons and the book would be complete. As it was the final chapter I'd given it much thought, researching it as well as I possibly could, and I had it all worked out. It would be a well-ordered chapter laying out precisely what the spiritual weapons are and how to use them. Then I'd bring the book to a climax and that would be that. Simple!

Well, it seems I was being somewhat rash! God knows that having it all meticulously laid out on paper with every 'i' dotted and 't' crossed is one thing, but that the outworking in a real live battle is quite another. Little did I know that God was about to catapult me into a situation that would require me to use every spiritual weapon I had ever been given. So in fact, this chapter hasn't exactly worked out in practice the way I would have originally written it. If I'm honest, it's nothing like it.

A dark night

It was the last Friday night before I finished this book, and fast approaching midnight. The boys had been in bed for a couple of hours and Helen and I were talking over a coffee with a friend called Jacky who was staying for the weekend. Suddenly, the living-room door opened. It was Nathan, but most unusually for our tall, fit fifteen-year-old, he was crying. He had his hands on his head and was in obvious distress. He said he had a severe pain in his head and it was getting worse.

It was clear that he needed immediate attention, so the first thing I did was lay hands on him and pray for him, and took him straight to hospital. It only took six minutes by car, but by now Nathan was literally writhing around in pain. Inside the hospital, the staff attended to him without delay. They put him in a side cubicle where he lay covered by a blanket while a flurry of activity went on around him. Doctors and nurses did all the necessary tests—they could see that this was not a normal headache.

Then they left us in the cubicle. We were in near darkness—it was better that way because light only seemed to aggravate the pain, which was constant and getting worse. Nathan was tossing and turning, crying and moaning—turning onto one side, then onto his back, then onto his other side, desperate to find a comfortable position. He'd sit up holding his head in his hands and then lie back down. Wrestling with his agony, he simply didn't know what to do with himself.

It was then that I realised that the giants were trying to crush us in their grip. For Nathan, these were obviously the giants of Pain and Sickness, but for me the giants that towered above were Fear, Panic and Out-of-proportion. They seemed to distort everything, insisting on telling me what might be wrong with our son and what might happen. Not only that, the giants Accusation and Guilt were telling me it was all my fault. Somehow I was to blame. I kept thinking 'If anything happens to him I'll never forgive myself!'—for what I didn't know, but that didn't stop me thinking it!

I tried to comfort Nathan as best I could, but I felt helpless. It has got to be one of the hardest things in the world for a parent to watch a suffering child, not knowing what to do. I was out of my head with worry and I felt like crying.

But there's a time for crying and a time for praying and this was definitely no time for the former. And all of a sudden, that verse of Scripture raced through my mind: 'The weapons of our warfare are not carnal but mighty through God to the pulling down of strongholds' (2 Cor 10:4).

This was definitely a battle—a time for employing every spiritual weapon at my disposal. If anyone should know about them it was me—after all, wasn't I writing a book with a whole chapter given over to the subject of spiritual weapons? The thing was, it wasn't that easy. The practice somehow wasn't matching the ordered theory I'd had in my mind earlier that day. However, I began the best way I could.

At first it was difficult just breaking through the worry and anxiety. There was no systematic, military plan of action—I simply threw at the devil and his frightening giants everything I could, in every way that I could. My mind was doing overtime trying to recall the various weapons—I felt so out of practice!

Out come the weapons

The first thing I did was to lay hands on Nathan again according to Mark 16:18, and I prayed the prayer of faith as best I knew how.

Then I turned to the word of God. My mouth became like a verbal machine gun, repeating every verse of Scripture I knew, as fast as I could. (In fact, in the heat of it all, I think I might have made up a few of my own as well!)

... greater is he that is in me than he that is in the world.

... if God be for us who can be against us?

... with his stripes we are healed.

... no weapon formed against us can prosper and no word can stand.

... without faith it is impossible to please God. But those that come to him must believe that he is, and that he rewards those who diligently seek him.

... with God all things are possible.

... where two or three agree on earth as touching anything it shall be done.

God is our refuge and strength, a very present help in times of trouble.

He sent the word and healed them.

And so I continued. I just kept praying as much Scripture as I knew over Nathan. At the time, however, I couldn't help thinking, 'I wish I knew more.'

I was also constantly using the weapon of prayer. I prayed in the name of Jesus. I prayed a hedge around the boy. I prayed with understanding and I prayed in tongues in the Spirit. I prayed to bind Satan and sickness, and to loose health into Nathan's body, following Matthew 18:18, where Jesus says '. . . whatever you bind on earth will be bound in heaven, and whatever you loose on earth will be loosed in heaven.' The word 'bind' here literally means 'prohibit' and I prayed all I could in Jesus' name, prohibiting the pain.

But then, of course, giant Doubt appeared. I suddenly thought of all those testimonies you hear of American preachers, people of faith, who have such authority, praying in faith through difficult situations and in an instant seeing the situation change. How I hoped this would happen now! But if anything, the more I prayed the worse Nathan's pain got. Doubt grew and mocked at me. But I still continued—speaking with my spiritual gift of tongues; and every so often, between moans and shrieks of pain, Nathan would join in with me.

Then I focused on pleading the blood of Christ. I have always believed passionately that there is power in the blood, so I prayed in faith, symbolically covering Nathan in the blood of our sacrificed Lord. I said, 'Lord, you died for Nathan and you shed your blood at Calvary for him. You not only took his sin, but you took all his sickness and pain as well.' Revelation 12:11 tells us, 'We overcome by the blood of the Lamb and the word of our testimony.' So I pleaded the blood; the testimony came later.

Then I started to praise—praise is a mighty spiritual weapon. The devil loathes our praise to God and so do his giants. I started giving God all the glory and thanking him for the victory as I started to sing with my spirit.

Mind you, all the time giant Worry and his partners in crime were still on my shoulder and Nathan was still battling in torturous pain. But the more I used the weapons, the more faith began to rise; I was getting a measure of authority. I have to say, though, I was also constantly thinking, 'I wish I was more proficient and skilful at using the weapons God has given me.'

To the ward

Having been in that darkened cubicle for more than two hours, Nathan was then taken down the long corridors of the hospital, up in a lift, and on to a ward. I followed that hospital trolley, praying every step of the way, and eventually we came to ward 26, where there was another flurry of activity and more tests.

Once we were alone again, I spent a further three or four hours flinging everything I'd got against the devil. And as time went on, the pain at last began to subside and Nathan became a lot calmer. I started to think about that verse in Revelation again, and remembered that conquest also comes by 'the word our testimony'. I wanted to utilise every conceivable weapon, so I thought, 'The next person who comes through that door is definitely going to hear my testimony one way or another!'

A few minutes later a nurse came in saying she needed to ask some routine questions. I told her all she needed to know, and then I started sharing with her about the things of God and some of the things Jesus has done in my life. Interestingly, she not only listened but she began asking serious questions about becoming a Christian and going to church.

And suddenly I just knew this was a God-ordained conversation. So I encouraged her in the way of Christ, and eventually she left and I carried on exactly where I'd left off, standing on the promises of God and calling on his name in a no-holds-barred, all-out war against the forces of darkness.

An important digression

I was so glad that night that I knew Jesus and that he was with me, and even more that Nathan knew him too. It made me wonder just how other people cope in such situations. I mean, unless a person consciously walks with God and knows Jesus personally, how do they get through? Jesus is such a refuge, 'a very present help in times of trouble'. But if a person doesn't know him, who else is there to turn to?

If you are reading this book and you have already invited Jesus into your life, you'll know what I'm talking about. Great! Pass it on!

But if you haven't invited Jesus to be your personal Saviour, if you've never said sorry and received forgiveness for your sins, if you've never accepted his love and the brand new start that comes with it, then you really are missing out. For Jesus Christ is unquestionably the one who can help you through. He will be your closest companion, sticking closer than any relative or friend. He cares for you so much and loves you with all he has and is. He proved it by dying on the cross for you so he could deal with the sin problem in your life, and destroy the works of the evil giants in your life. At Calvary he overcame every conceivable giant—and that includes yours.

But also, when Jesus rose again, he defeated the

biggest giant of all, giant Death. And because he has conquered death, so can you and I. And because he lives again, so also can you and I. He really does want to save you and be your Lord, to be your closest companion and guide, to fight on your behalf and be your own giant-killer. And it's all just for the asking.

What do I mean, all for the asking? Well, Jesus really is courtesy itself. He never barges in and gate-crashes people's lives. He only comes when invited. You must willingly invite him to be at the centre of your life and then, and only then, will you truly become a child of God. It really is important to do this. Believe me, you will never regret it.

Back to the ward

By now I was beginning to notice something interesting: the more I utilised my spiritual weapons, the more proficient I was becoming at using them. Six hours later, Nathan was also feeling semi-normal again. After further observation, he was given some medication and the all-clear, and discharged pain-free. Praise God! In fact, no one seemed to be able to say exactly what the problem had been; it may have been a severe migraine attack, though he'd never had one before— or since, for that matter. But whatever it actually was, it certainly caused me to pull out all my spiritual weaponry.

Now I'm not saying, use these weapons and people's sickness will always disappear. That would be stupid and ignore the experience of many people of great faith whose relatives have died of tragic illnesses. What I'm saying is, when you use God's spiritual weaponry, he really will deliver you from your giants—of fear, panic, worry, doubt, or whatever. When we finally left, I thought, 'O God, thank you for the practical weapons, the hospital, the doctors and nurses and medics, their knowledge, and all that goes with it. But even more than that, thank you for your spiritual weapons so generously given to us. They really can pull down strongholds!'

My friend, take hold of these weapons, and make them yours, for they are yours by right.

Twelve key weapons

Let's just recap on the spiritual weapons at our disposal. We all need to study them, learn them, and practise them; and when we do it will stand us in good stead—for who knows when we'll be flung into battle? I have listed a few key scriptures to help your progress because these are definitely the weapons with which to slay your giants.

Weapon no. 1 Knowing Jesus

The prerequisite for winning any spiritual battle is knowing Jesus personally. The giants hate Jesus for they know he defeated them through his death and resurrection. Your personal relationship with Jesus and having him as Lord of your life is the greatest of all the weapons you will ever have.

See: John 3:1–21; Ephesians 2:8–10; Philippians 3:10–12; 1 John 1:7–9; 1 John 5:20.

Weapon no. 2 The Word of God

Reading, studying, meditating on, confessing, living by and standing on the promises of the word of God is a vital weapon. It will never let you down.

See: Deuteronomy 28:1–14; Joshua 1:8–9; Psalm 19:7–11;
Luke 4:32; Hebrews 4:12; James 1:22–24.

Weapon no. 3 *Prayer*

This is a top priority for every day. The devil simply
cannot cope with you being a prayer warrior—he has
no counter-weapon. Prayer stands on its own.

See: 2 Chronicles 7:14; Matthew 21:21–22; Mark 11:24;
Ephesians 6:18; 1 Timothy 4:5; James 5: 16–18.

Weapon no. 4 *Speaking and praying in tongues*

Speaking and praying in tongues is a mighty weapon.
Too many Christians think it's just a gift to pull out at
one's own convenience—for 'display' purposes even!
Too few use it as an active weapon on a daily basis,
but that's what the gift was given to us for.

See: Acts 2; Ephesians 6:18; 1 Corinthians 14:14–16, 18.

Weapon no. 5 *The name of Jesus*

The name of Jesus is supremely powerful. 'At the
name of Jesus, every knee must bow and every
tongue confess that he is Lord.' Demons tremble at
his name and every giant must bow down.

See: Matthew 6:9; Mark 16:15–20; Philippians 2:9–10.

Weapon no. 6 *The blood of Christ*

At a fundamental level the blood of Christ is the key
to it all. We are saved, redeemed, forgiven, justified
and have access to the throne room of God by the
blood of Jesus Christ shed on the cross for us. It is
through Christ's blood that we overcome the devil. It
is through Christ's blood that we become complete.

See: Exodus 12; Colossians 1:20; Hebrews 9; 1 Peter 1:19; Revelation 12:11.

Weapon no. 7 Your testimony and the fruits of the Holy Spirit

Revelation 12:11 tells us that we overcome the evil one 'through the blood of the Lamb and the word of our testimony'. Our daily testimony—in other words, the way we live—is vitally important. It's not just a case of talking the talk, we've got to walk the walk. To do this, we need the fruit of the Holy Spirit: love, joy, peace, patience, kindness, goodness, faithfulness, gentleness and self-control. God sees these as mega-important. We need to walk exactly as Jesus walked.

See: John 4:4–30; Ephesians 4:1–3, 26–27; Galatians 5:22–23; 1 John 2:6.

Weapon no. 8 The laying on of hands

God's word instructs us to use the laying on of hands. Some people argue that this isn't really a weapon, but I profoundly believe it is. In fact the Scripture tells us that at times it is crucial.

See: Mark 16:17–20; Acts 18:18; James 5:13–16; 1 Timothy 4:14.

Weapon no. 9 Faith

Hebrews 11:6 is very clear. It tells us that it is impossible to please God without faith. Everything we have is through faith and that includes obtaining victory in any situation.

See: Mark 11:22–24; 2 Corinthians 5:7; Matthew 9; Hebrews 11; Romans 4; 10:17; 1 John 5:4.

Weapon no. 10 *Praise*

In the Old Testament it wasn't uncommon for the tribe of Judah to lead the way into battle. The people in this tribe were the praisers, the musicians, the worshippers. They used praise as a real weapon in declaring victory.

See: 2 Chronicles 20:21; Isaiah 61:1–3; Matthew 6:9–13.

Weapon no. 11 *Perseverance*

Each one of us is destined to win, so we really have got to develop a mindset and a tenacity to do this for God. Paul tells us to 'fight the good fight' (1 Tim 6:12) so let's make sure we fight it! Keep on keeping on, and you'll slay every giant!

See: 1 Corinthians 15:58; Galatians 6:7–9; 1 Thessalonians 5:24; Hebrews 6:12; 11:6; James 1:4.

Weapon no. 12 *The full armour of God*

Many Christians have struggled because they've tried to streak their way into heaven! They've got on the helmet of salvation, but where's the rest of their armour?! Ephesians 6:10–18 instructs us to put on 'the whole armour of God [not just part of it] that we may be able to stand against the wiles of the devil'.

The interesting thing about the armour as described in Ephesians is that there was nothing to cover a person's back. Could this be because we are never to turn our back on our enemies, but always face them fair and square and defeat them once and for all?

See: Isaiah 59:16–19; Romans 13:12–14; 1 Peter 5:8–9.

The time is right

Now is the time to stand up and trust God. I once heard someone say, 'If we have all these weapons, why is it all such a battle?' Well, I guess it's a bit like soap—completely useless just sitting on the shelf, and going quite hard and cracked if not used for a long time. Weapons, too, are only effective when they're used, and used often. So don't shrink back from your giant. Pick up those weapons and face it! The quicker you do, the quicker you will have the victory.

The forty-first of the month

Throughout this book we have talked a lot about that fascinating Old Testament character, David. We've seen how God chose him when no one else gave him a second look. We saw how he walloped Goliath. And if we looked some more, we'd see what an enormous number of other phenomenal battles in which this shepherd-king was victorious.

Now I want you to imagine you're giving David an interview, and in it you ask him to share some of the highlights of his life. He might begin by recalling the days he killed the bear that attacked his sheep, and how he slew a lion on another occasion. No doubt he'd remember the day he was anointed as king. He might talk with great jubilation about that memorable coronation day, when he sat on his throne and began to reign. He might wax eloquent about the many victorious battles he led, and in particular he might recall that day, long before, when he slew Goliath and delivered the whole of Israel. He might flush with pride to remember how his prize on that occasion had been the hand of the king's daughter—a princess, no less. Not bad for a young lad who'd started out one day as an odd-job, fill-in sandwich carrier.

For forty days the Israelites had been tormented. But then came the day of victory. What a difference a day made—just twenty-four hours. And do you know what? A couple of days ago I found myself wondering when that momentous action of David's actually happened. Was it a Monday—a boring old, get-back-to-the-grindstone day? Was it a Friday, as it was when Nathan was dashed to hospital? Was it maybe over the weekend?

As I was thinking this, I felt God say to me: 'Phil, do you want to know exactly when it was?'

'Yes please,' I answered, and he told me.

'It was the forty-first of the month.'

I didn't understand at first, and then I did. The forty-first day was the one the situation turned around. It was the day of victory.

Now in the Scriptures, 'forty days' crops up a lot:

- It rained for forty days and Noah was desperate. The forty-first day, the sun came out.
- Jesus spent forty days in the wilderness. The forty-first day, he returned with a new anointing, ready to defeat all giants—with God, his loving Father.
- For forty days, Moses' deputies spied out the Promised Land. The forty-first day, Caleb and Joshua gave their great report: 'Surely we can take the land.'
- There's also this wonderful day when David slew Goliath. The Israelites had suffered forty days of abject misery, with Goliath flaunting himself at

them and hurling one threat after another. The forty-first day, a single pebble from a boy who trusted the Lord killed him stone dead.

- And of course Lent is the forty-day period when many people remember the sufferings and passion of our Lord Jesus Christ. On the forty-first day, we celebrate his glorious resurrection. Hallelujah!

Slay your giant

Take heart. Every one of us has a 'forty-day' patch from time to time. Sometimes the patch can last for months or even years—like the Israelites in the desert. Sometimes you think it will never end. Sometimes it's so hard, you'd prefer to be out of it completely. Who wouldn't?

But there is a day of victory. There is a resurrection day coming. We are born 'for such a time as this' (Esther 4:14), and the truth is that God is just waiting to give us a forty-first day victory experience. So make it yours today. And if anyone asks you the date, tell them it's the forty-first of the month—giant-killing day.

Now go and slay that giant!